'There must be some mistake.'

'Perhaps there were two candidates—Janie and Jamie are very similar——'

'So they might be, but I'm Jamie, with an "m"—you know, for monkey?'

'Not nuts?' Rob said with an unexpected touch of humour.

Her lips twitched. 'Not until I got here!'

Dear Reader

When you behave out of character, it is sure to find you out, as Sharon Wirdnam's heroine discovers in SURGEON OF THE HEART. And when trust has been abused, it is hard to accept love again, as Rob finds out in A GENTLE GIANT from Caroline Anderson. We go to Italy in Lisa Cooper's DREAM OF NAPLES, and explore the role of alternative medicine in HAND IN HAND with Margaret Barker. Happy holidays!

The Editor

Caroline Anderson's nursing career was brought to an abrupt halt by a back injury, but her interest in medical things led her to work first as a medical secretary, and then, after completing her teacher training, as a lecturer in medical office practice to trainee medical secretaries. In addition to writing, she also runs her own business from her home in rural Suffolk, where she lives with her husband, two daughters, mother and dog.

Recent titles by the same author:

MORE THAN TIME
SAVING DR GREGORY

A GENTLE GIANT

BY

CAROLINE ANDERSON

MILLS & BOON LIMITED
ETON HOUSE 18–24 PARADISE ROAD
RICHMOND SURREY TW9 1SR

First published in Great Britain 1992
by Mills & Boon Limited

This edition 1992

ISBN 0 263 77814 2

Set in 10 on 12 pt Linotron Times
03-9208-50193

Typeset in Great Britain by Centracet, Cambridge
Made and printed in Great Britain

CHAPTER ONE

IT WAS a stone house, painted white like all the others, but large in comparison with its neighbours. Flowering shrubs nestled against the garden walls, their leaves still damp after the rain, and the intoxicating fragrance of night-scented stocks and nicotiana drifted on the mild evening air.

Jamie paused, her hand on the knocker, and listened to the stillness. She could hear the steady throb of a distant fishing boat, and the harsh cries of the gulls wheeling at the stern as the boat chugged steadily up the loch. Nearer to hand she caught the intermittent laugh of a little child, and the happy sound brought a soft smile to her lips.

It was so different from the city—so different, and so clean! No noisy crowds, no overflowing litterbins and gangs of youths hanging around every street corner. This small community, snuggled down in the fold of the land with the sea at its front and the mountains at its back, was a place where people worked hard and honestly. It looked clean and decent, a new beginning—and she was more than ready for it.

She straightened her skirt, smoothed her honey-gold curls into some semblance of order and drew a deep, sweet-smelling breath of fresh sea air. The smile still lingering around her soft blue eyes, Jamie turned back to the door and banged on the knocker. She heard the sound reverberate round the hall, and then quick footsteps approached.

'Hello, there—come away in, would you, I'm just on the phone. Is it Dr Buchanan you'd be after?'

Jamie nodded agreement at the pleasant, middle-aged woman. 'That's right—I'm——'

'You'll find him in the room on the left at the end—go on through, hen. I must get back to the phone. Can you manage?'

'Of course,' Jamie said softly to the woman's retreating back, and headed quietly down the hall.

'On the left,' she murmured to herself, and, just as she reached the end of the corridor, a tiny child, vest flapping round her chubby legs, came barrelling round the corner, shrieking with laughter. A diminutive cherub, Jamie thought as the baby giggled again and waddled past her, her glossy black curls bouncing around her flushed cheeks.

'I'm going to get you!' growled a deep voice, and a huge bear of a man on hands and knees came charging round the corner snarling and snapping his teeth, and ground to a halt at Jamie's feet. He looked up, his head level with her thighs, and gave a quiet groan.

'Ah—er—hello!' He stood up, brushing off his knees, and as he straightened, Jamie took a step back. He was *huge*! At five foot six, Jamie was used to men a little taller than her, although in high heels she could look many of her male colleagues in the eye. But this man! She didn't even reach the dark-shadowed chin that jutted above her! Nor was he simply tall. He was broad, solid and vigorously masculine to boot.

He was also acutely embarrassed.

'Sorry about that,' he mumbled, a dull flush mounting his craggy cheeks. 'Let me just catch the wee scamp and I'll be with you. Chloe? Come here, darling——'

He squeezed past her and strode down the corridor. There was a delighted shriek, and the sound of an enormous raspberry, and then the man reappeared, apologising again. 'That's better; Mrs H has got her now. Come on in to the surgery.' He led her down the corridor to the room opposite the one from which he had emerged, and opened the door for her, ushering her in with a hand on the small of her back.

It was impossible to go through the door without brushing against him, and, as she did so, Jamie felt the solidity of his body with a sensation of shock. He was built like granite, huge and unyielding, but unlike granite he radiated warmth and energy.

She felt at once safe and threatened, and for the life of her she couldn't work out why. All she knew was that he had a physical presence, unrelated to his size, that something deep inside her had recognised, and she felt as if all the air had been sucked out of her lungs.

She took a deep breath and looked around, and was immediately captivated by her surroundings. The surgery was painted white, the plain walls hung with bold pencil drawings, delicate watercolours and children's daubs in equal proportion. Mixed in among the colourful display were the more usual posters about breastfeeding and smoking. One of the amateurish paintings caught her eye.

In it a bright and vigorous sun shone cheerfully on a picture-book cottage, and a raggy tortoiseshell cat perched on the wall outside. 'Dear Dr Rob,' the straggling inscription read, 'I'm better now. I love you. Trudy.'

'Who's Trudy?' she asked with a smile.

She had thought he was ugly, has face too rugged for good looks, his heavy brows and battered nose no adornment to the rough-hewn plains and valleys of his cheeks above the jutting jaw. Then he smiled, and the sun lit up his midnight eyes and scattered in a million rays from the corners, and the brackets round his mouth deepened as a slow chuckle rose from his chest. Goodness, she thought, why ever did I think he was ugly? She had to force herself to take a breath.

'A young fan,' he admitted gently. 'A real treasure, bless her.'

He closed the door and moved round behind the vast mahogany desk. 'Take a seat. What can I do for you?'

She continued to stand, the lingering traces of a smile touching her eyes, and held out her hand. 'I'm Jamie Cameron—I believe you're expecting me.'

An expression of puzzlement crossed his face, and then he let out his breath on a harsh rush of disbelief.

'Who?'

Her smile slipped, and she retrieved her hand from the air over his desk and tucked it into her jacket pocket. 'Jamie Cameron. You *were* expecting me?'

'No—that is, I was expecting a Dr Cameron, but I certainly wasn't expecting *you*!'

'Pardon?'

'You're a woman,' he said accusingly.

She glanced down at herself and blinked. 'So I am. How astonishing!'

He glowered at her.

'Is that a problem?'

'A problem?' he growled. 'Are you joking?'

She lost the last of her smile. 'Dr Buchanan, I can't pretend to understand, but I can assure you I have in my bag a letter from you asking me to join you in the practice, initially for a trial period——'

'Not you,' he insisted. 'There must be some mistake. Perhaps there were two candidates—Janie and Jamie are very similar——'

'So they might be, but I'm Jamie, with an "m"—you know, for monkey?'

'Not nuts?' he said with an unexpected touch of humour.

Her lips twitched. 'Not until I got here!'

His eyes swept her fleetingly, as if to check that she was indeed a woman, and he dropped heavily into his chair with a sigh. He muttered something under his breath that she pretended not to hear, and then he shot back the chair and strode over to the filing cabinet.

Yanking out a file, he returned to the desk and slapped the file down amid the papers that littered its surface. Several of them drifted off the edge of the desk and she bent to retrieve them. His finger traced down the application form to the M/F question, and stabbed the circled F viciously.

'Oh, God, bloody hell. Why didn't I see it before?' he said bitterly.

She straightened up and glanced round at the chaos. 'Perhaps because you were rushed off your feet and barely able to cope?' she suggested gently.

'More than likely,' he muttered brusquely. 'That's

why I wasn't at the interview. Damn! Another wait. Oh, well, it can't be helped——'

'Wait? What are you talking about?'

He slapped the file shut and pushed away from the desk, propping his huge feet on the edge. 'You can't stay. Surely you can see that?'

She shook her head. Maybe the ten-hour drive had affected her mind, but she didn't think so. 'I don't see that at all. I'm perfectly qualified to do the job!'

He cranked an eyebrow. 'On paper, maybe.'

She took a deep breath. 'Tell me, Dr Buchanan, how many suitable applicants did you have?'

He sighed and ran his hand through the tangle of black locks that fell forward over his brow. 'Only you,' he admitted reluctantly, but he met her eyes frankly. 'You were the only suitably qualified applicant stupid enough to want to work out here in the wilds of nowhere who had enough money to invest in the practice and no overriding need to escape from the world. That's why you were offered the job. That, and because I thought with a name like yours you would be a Scotsman with some understanding of the country.'

'And would you have put my application forward if you'd realised I was a woman?' she asked quietly.

He met her eye without a qualm. 'No way. This is no place for a girl.'

'Rubbish! Lots of women live out here quite happily!' She stressed the word 'women' slightly but deliberately. His gaze flicked over her, and returned to her eyes.

'They're raised to it. You aren't. You belong in the

city, Dr Cameron, not the wilds of Scotland. You aren't safe here.'

She gave a harsh, bitter laugh. 'Dr Buchanan, I did my GP trainee year in an inner-city practice. In one month alone my flat was burgled three times and I was mugged and almost raped while I was making a night visit. You call that safe?'

He gave her a level look. 'There are different types of safety. Up here, you get into difficulties in the snow and good men are going to risk their lives to help you.'

'And they wouldn't help you? What if you got stuck in the snow?'

'I wouldn't.'

'Superman, eh?' She snorted. 'God deliver me from arrogant male chauvinists!'

'If I have my way, He will,' Dr Buchanan muttered, reaching for the phone. Two seconds later he slammed the receiver back down and growled something unintelligible.

'I beg your pardon?'

'Sunday,' he said succinctly. 'There'll be nobody there.' He glared at her for a moment or two, and then, as if he had made up his mind about something, he unfolded his long body and stood up. 'I've got two calls to make. You might as well come with me, then you'll get some idea of what we're up against. Perhaps it'll put you off.'

'Don't hold your breath,' she muttered.

His craggy brows shot up. 'What?'

'I said that will be very nice.' Ignoring her pounding head and the crick in her back from the long day behind the wheel, she rose calmly to her feet and followed him. He went into an office that was marginally more chaotic than the surgery, and retrieved two sets of notes from the wall of patient files, then picking up a battered old medical bag in one hand and his coat in the other, he held the door for her.

They met Mrs H in the hall, the dark-haired moppet in her arms. 'Another call for you, Doctor. Trudy's got a query again. I said you'd pop in and have a look.'

He dropped a kiss on the baby's head, tousled the soft curls and went back into the surgery. When he emerged, he gave Jamie a thoughtful look. 'Have you arranged accommodation yet?'

She shook her head. 'I thought I'd book into the pub until I'd found somewhere to rent——'

Mrs H tutted disapprovingly, and Dr Buchanan turned to the housekeeper. 'Mrs Harrison, Dr Cameron will be staying the night. I wonder if you could make up a bed for her in the spare room? I'll take the phone—contact me if any more calls come through.'

With that he kissed the baby again, opened the front door and ushered Jamie out into the still evening. She breathed in the heady scent of the flowers, and followed him to a battered old Land Rover standing in the drive.

'Why do you feel the need to control people?' she asked loudly as they roared off down the road in a great cloud of diesel fumes.

He looked puzzled. 'Control who?' he yelled.

'Me! I would have been quite happy in the pub, but you obviously have this absurd moralistic and chauvinistic attitude towards women——'

'It's shut.'

'What?'

'The pub. It's shut. Sunday. With the best will in the world you couldn't have stayed there tonight, and anyway they don't do accommodation.'

'Well, I could have found a guest house——'

'No chance. It's September.'

She gave an exasperated sigh and ran her fingers through her tangled hair. 'Would you care to elaborate?'

He shot her a grin. 'Sure. Shooting season. The place is overrun with guns.'

'Oh.' Suitably chastened, she fell silent for a while, and then her professional curiosity got the better of her. 'Who are you going to visit?'

'Elderly woman who's had a fall and may have a fracture, and a woman who thinks she's in labour prematurely.'

'And Trudy.'

'Aye, and Trudy,' he said softly—so softly that she wouldn't have caught it if she hadn't been watching him.

'Tell me about her,' Jamie prompted.

A whole series of emotions played across his face, and then he sighed. 'She's eight. She got glomerulonephritis from a neglected strep throat, and ended up with chronic renal failure. To make matters worse her mother's disabled. It made Trudy's dialysis difficult, because Mum can't drive and they can't afford a home dialysis unit. She's missed so much school, and become so exhausted with all the travelling, that they've switched her to CAPD—continuous ambulatory peritoneal dialysis. So far she's doing really well, but every now and then she gets a touch of peritonitis and we all panic for a bit until it settles down.'

'Isn't she very young for that? I mean, changing the fluid all the time and so on—does her mother do it for her?'

He shook his head. 'No. Trudy virtually runs the house, and all her CAPD procedure is handled by her. Her mother's always there, but I get the feeling Trudy is the one who does the bulk of it. She's so gutsy, it makes you weep.' He gave a self-conscious laugh, and flashed her a grin. 'She's a great kid, but what she needs is a transplant.'

'What about one of her family donating a kidney?' Jamie asked. 'If it was my child, I wouldn't hesitate. I assume no one is suitable?'

'There's only her mother, and she's got MS. It makes her a rather unsuitable donor!'

'Oh, good grief, the poor child!'

'Mmm. Exactly.'

They travelled in silence for a while, each absorbed in thoughts, and Jamie was able to look at her surroundings. Dusk was falling as they approached a lonely cottage on a tiny, winding track.

He braked to a halt outside the cottage and jumped out. 'You might as well come in,' he said briskly, and went inside. She followed him slowly, her legs stiffening up after the long day, and found him crouched on the floor in front of a frail little lady, her tiny wrist lying oddly in his great hand.

Jamie noticed that it had the classic 'dinner-fork' appearance of a Colles' fracture.

'You've done it again, my darling, haven't you?' he said softly, one finger lightly brushing the back of her gnarled hand. 'You'll have to go to the hospital for an X-ray, and then they'll set it for you and put it in plaster.'

'I thought you'd say that, so I packed a bag and arranged for my neighbour to feed the cats. Do I have to go? I hate that place, it's so noisy. Can't you set it, Doctor?'

'Not really, my love. You'd be better off in the hospital, truly. I'll put a splint on it so it doesn't hurt you, and then we'll call the ambulance and they can come and get you.' He laid her hand gently back in her lap, and stood up, his head bowed to clear the low ceiling. 'I tell you what, I'll do a deal with you. You promise not to do this again, and I'll send you to the cottage hospital instead of Fort William. How's that?' he said with a wink, and the woman laughed.

'I'll do my best just for you, you handsome devil!'

He gave a cheeky grin. 'That's what all the ladies tell me!'

While he went out to the Land Rover for the splint and then phoned the hospital, Jamie introduced herself and admired the patchwork that was sticking out of a basket in the corner.

'I do them all the time—well, with no television there's not a lot to keep me out of mischief——'

'They'll be here in a minute. That'll keep you out of mischief for a day or so. Let's get this splint on.'

Jamie watched as he dealt tenderly with the broken limb. For such a big man he was incredibly gentle, his large hands surprisingly deft. She couldn't take her eyes off him.

She was caught staring, of course. He lifted his head and met her eyes and an eyebrow quirked mockingly at her.

'Never seen a splint put on?' he ribbed gently, and she flushed.

'Of course I have!' she muttered defensively, and he laughed.

'Of course. There you are, Mrs McKay. All done.'

A few moments later the ambulance arrived to take her to the cottage hospital, and they set off again.

'Where to now?'

'Mrs Reeve—baby's not due until the middle of October, but she's had a show and the odd twinge. I said I'd look in, and luckily it's not far away, then it's back to Trudy.'

A short while later they turned off the main road on to a bumpy farm track, and bounced and jostled along for about a mile before reaching the isolated croft at the end.

'What a lovely place to live!' she exclaimed, gazing round at the broad swaths of heather and grass dotted with sheep and bathed with gold by the slanting rays of evening sun.

'You think so? Of course it's very pretty in September, but in January it's quite different. They can be cut off for weeks at a time.'

He was only trying to put her off, she realised, so she ignored his comment.

'Can I come in?'

'Only if you promise not to stare,' he told her, and she blushed again.

'I wasn't staring. There was nothing else to look at!'

He grinned. 'Don't mind me. I'm just not used to being watched all the time. Of course you can come in.'

He led the way, introducing her to Mr Reeve, a tall, solid young man in his late twenties.

'I expect you'll want to wash your hands,' he said to Rob, and the doctor went over to the sink in the corner of the living-room-cum-kitchen, stripped off his coat and scrubbed thoroughly.

The shepherd handed him a towel, and then opened a door. 'Josie's in bed,' he told them, and they followed him out to the back of the little single-storey cottage. 'Doctor's here, hen,' he said gently, and the woman turned her head and smiled sleepily, pushing herself into a sitting position.

'Sorry, Doctor, I dozed off. Thank you for coming. I'm sorry to call you out—it's probably nothing, but I just felt I ought to check.'

He smiled reassuringly. 'That's what I'm here for, Mrs Reeve. Let's have a look, can I?'

The woman eased back down the bed, and he pulled back the covers and felt her abdomen all over, his huge hands all but covering it.

'How often are the contractions?'

'Half an hour or so—nothing very bad, but they were stronger than the others, the practice ones you told me about—oh, there's one starting!'

He kept his hands still, and then nodded. 'I'm fairly

sure they're still just the Braxton-Hicks, but if I can just take a look we'll be sure. What was the show like?'

'Just a slight pink stain—nothing much, but I didn't know what to expect.'

'More than that, probably, but not everybody has one.' He flipped open his bag, pulled on a pair of gloves and examined her deftly while her husband shifted awkwardly near the door. Jamie smiled at him.

'It's lovely here, isn't it?' she said quietly.

He seemed relieved to be given something else to focus on. 'Aye, we love it. Couldn't live anywhere else. Can't stand the city.'

She grinned. 'Neither can I—dirty, stinking place. Give me the country any day of the week.'

She turned back to Mrs Reeve, who was now respectable again.

The doctor was stripping off his gloves and shrugging back into his jacket. 'No problem. Your cervix hasn't started to open yet, as I thought, but I doubt you'll be long. That's a fair old baby you've got there, you know.'

She smiled. 'Takes after Sandy, I expect,' she said fondly.

'You're sure of your dates?'

'Oh, aye. There was only that one month, because the month before Sandy was away bringing the sheep in, and he was too tired. . .'

She flushed and trailed to a halt, and Dr Buchanan stifled a smile.

'Just try and rest a bit for a few days, and call me if you're the slightest bit worried. Don't worry about wasting my time. I'd rather be called too early than too late, all right? I'll see you on Tuesday at the clinic.'

As they walked back to the front of the house, Sandy took the doctor on one side and murmured something to him. Judging by the way he blushed and shifted from foot to foot, it was something he would rather Jamie didn't hear, so she took herself out to the Land Rover and waited there.

A few seconds later the doctor emerged, shook hands with the young shepherd and climbed up into the cab.

As they pulled away, a broad smile broke up his rugged features, and he turned to her, his eyes twinkling.

'He's had a quiet week on the farm, and they've been taking advantage of the fact to do a little honey-mooning. He wondered if he might have done her any harm!'

Jamie chuckled. 'Judging by his smile, you set his mind at rest!'

He nodded, and the smile faded. 'On that score, but I'm still concerned about the baby's size, and to a certain extent its position. The head's engaged, and all I can feel is hands and feet and bottom, So I think we may end up with a malpresentation. Of course there's nothing to stop it turning; it's still pretty active. I've told him to bring her in to the branch surgery on Tuesday and bring a urine sample—I just want to check she's not become diabetic during her pregnancy, but she hasn't got any of the other symptoms. It could be deceptive, of course, but I think I'll get her sent along to the hospital for a scan.'

Jamie's brow creased into a frown. 'Do you think she'll have problems with delivery, then?'

He shrugged. 'Could be. Her pelvis isn't bad, but that baby seemed big enough now, and she's still got six weeks to go.'

'Trudy next?'

'Uh-huh. That's back the way we've come and on a bit further.' They headed down the track, turned left at the end and made good speed along the narrow, twisting road back to the coast. Then they ran along beside the loch again, sometimes so near to the water that Jamie felt she could touch it. The darkness was creeping in, and with it her tiredness, but the peace and tranquillity took the edge off her discomfort and she relaxed back against the seat and closed her eyes.

Seconds later she was being shaken gently awake by a massive hand cupping her shoulder, and as she straightened she found herself inches away from his startling slate-grey eyes.

'I went to sleep—I'm sorry,' she said breathlessly, and he nodded slightly. 'It's the drive—I left early this morning.'

He nodded again. 'You should be tucked up in bed somewhere, not gadding about the countryside. We're at Trudy's house—do you want to come in, or stay here and rest?'

She looked around. They were parked outside a little terraced cottage in the middle of a village—if you could call it that. Out here, where neighbours were few and far between, a cluster of five or six houses probably did count as a village, Jamie thought, and it was here that Trudy lived.

'Come in?'

'Come on, then.'

He swung down from the seat, hefting his bag like a handful of feathers, and strode up to the door.

It was answered by a small girl who looked about seven at the most, but turned out to be Trudy, small for her age because of her temperamental health.

'Hello, Dr Rob!' she said with a gappy smile, and he ruffled her hair and hugged her against his side with one long arm.

'How's my girl, then? What's this I hear about you not feeling too good?'

'Oh, I feel fine, but I had jellyfish in my effluent and Mum though I ought to call you. I told her it was just fibrin, but she panics!'

Jamie stifled a grin, but Rob was dead-pan and serious.

'Did you save it for me to look at?'

'Of course!' She gave a cheeky grin and led the way through to the little sitting-room. 'Mum, Dr Rob's here. He's brought a visitor. Come away in and sit down. Would you like a cup of tea?'

'No, thank you. Trudy, come here and sit down and let me see this effluent. I expect Dr Cameron here would like to see it too. You're sure you feel quite well?'

'Uh-huh—I'll get it.'

She skipped off, and her mother gave a weary smile. 'She should be in bed by now, but I thought—I'd hate to neglect her and have anything dreadful go wrong. Like that sore throat—I'll never forgive myself for that, but she always had them, and I thought it was just one more. . .'

Rob laid a hand on her knee and squeezed gently. 'You had enough on your plate, Mrs Douglas. Your husband had just left you, your MS was progressing fast and furiously—no one could possibly blame you, and I'm damn sure Trudy doesn't. And I think you did the right thing to call me tonight. Ah, Trudy, let's see your jellyfish.'

He held up the bag of yellow-coloured fluid which had been used to dialyse Trudy, and frowned at it. 'You sure you haven't been fishing in the loch?'

She giggled. 'I fell in yesterday—maybe some of the jellyfish swam inside then!'

He lowered the bag. 'Did you fall in?'

'No, of course not! I was just teasing you.'

'Hmm. I'm never sure with you, young lady. Well, I reckon that's all right, but I think we need to have a look at you. Could you just lie down on the settee and let me see your tummy?'

Once again Jamie was fascinated, but this time by Trudy. Just beside her tummy-button was a neat little hole through which emerged a catheter with a connector on the end, linked to another length of tube that ran to an empty bag. The skin around the exit site was clean and pink and healthy, and Rob nodded and covered the little girl up.

'How's your weight?'

'Fine—going up a bit, but I've grown, so I think that must be why. I tried drinking less in case it was a fluid build-up but I got dehydrated——'

'Trudy, come and talk to me or the clinic before you alter your fluid intake, love.'

The child instantly looked crestfallen, and he sat beside her and engulfed her little hand in his.

'Trudy, I'm very proud of the way you've learnt to understand your condition and deal with all your problems, but there are times, and things, that you don't know enough about. You know, the health service pay me and the people in the CAPD clinic a lot of money to help people like you—it's cheating them if you won't let us!'

She looked up at him, her serious face melting into a loving smile. 'I didn't want to worry you. You always look so tired. . .' Her little hand came up and cupped his cheek, and he flushed slightly and hugged her.

'Don't you worry about me. I'm fine. Anyway, Dr Cameron here is going to help me for a little while. Let me take your temperature and blood-pressure. Any chest pain, swollen ankles or shortness of breath?'

She shook her head, temporarily silenced by the thermometer.

'Peaceful, isn't it?' Rob joked, and Trudy punched his arm gently.

He grinned and took the thermometer out of her mouth. 'Fine. Good. I'll put some heparin in the next couple of bags to keep the fibrin down, so it doesn't clog the tube, then I want to know if it comes back again or if the effluent quantity is down. OK?'

Trudy nodded sagely. 'Shall I ring the clinic?'

He tapped her on the end of her nose. 'No, madam, you shall not, I'll do it. I'll see you again in a day or two. Now, how about going to bed?'

He was quiet on the way back to the surgery, and so was Jamie. In fact, she was too shocked and moved to speak, her thoughts trapped by the tremendous courage of the little girl whose life was destined to be dominated by her dialysis. Over and over again medicine had shown her the vast resources of courage that people, and especially children, were able to tap in times of crisis. It was humbling, and awe-inspiring, and just then it made her want to cry.

She huddled down in the seat and turned her face to the window, staring out into the almost dark night. Although it was late, the night was clear and bright, the moon gleaming coldly on the rocks by the shore. It was a night for lovers, she thought sadly, a night made for strolling hand in hand—not for sitting beside a man who had made it clear he had no use for her.

She risked a quick glance at his stern profile, and swallowed. He looked angry—furiously so, and she wondered why.

'She needs a transplant,' he growled. 'Poor bloody kid shouldn't have to suffer like that! It makes me so cross—the number of people who die with perfectly healthy kidneys, and because they haven't thought of carrying a donor card, a kid like Trudy is condemned to an abbreviated lifetime of constant dialysis.'

'She's got time,' Jamie murmured soothingly. 'Perhaps a kidney will turn up soon.'

'Maybe.'

He turned the Land Rover on to the drive and cut the engine, and the quiet of the night stole over them, A dog was barking somewhere in the distance, and they sat for a moment absorbing the stillness. Then the front door was opened and a golden flood spilled out into the garden.

'Call for you, Doctor. Mrs McRae—think's she's got a chest infection. And the babe won't settle without a kiss from her father.'

He grinned. 'I'll give her won't settle. Call Mrs McRae for me and tell her I'm coming, and I'll sort Chloe out.'

He was in, upstairs, back down and off out again within five minutes. Mrs H took Jamie upstairs and showed her her room and the bathroom which she would share with the housekeeper and the baby.

'Dr Buchanan's got his own bathroom off his bedroom, so we're quite private. I expect you'd like a bath and then something to eat, wouldn't you? You look all in.'

Jamie agreed, and bathed quickly, dressing warmly in a tracksuit before running back downstairs. She found the kitchen by trial and error, and Mrs H turned to her with a smile.

'Here you are, lass. Bacon and mushroom omelette and a cup of tea.'

Jamie returned the smile. 'Thank you, you're very kind. How did you know I was hungry?'

There was a motherly chuckle. 'I didn't, but it was a fair bet that you hadn't eaten before you got here, and the doctor wouldn't have given it a thought. If it wasn't for me tying him down and force-feeding him three times a day, that man wouldn't eat from one week's end to the next.'

'What about his wife?' Jamie asked, and the housekeeper's face lost its smile.

'Away,' she said briefly.

'On holiday?'

She snorted. 'You could say that.'

'Oh.' Jamie didn't quite know what to make of that. 'When's she coming back?'

There was a slight sound behind her, and she turned, the blood draining from her face. She had never seen anyone look so angry in her entire life. Then he turned on his heel and slammed the door behind him.

She turned her bemused gaze back to the housekeeper, and the woman sank down at the table and covered Jamie's hand. 'Don't let him frighten you—and don't let him drive you away either. If ever a man needed help it's that one.'

'Tell me about his wife,' Jamie pleaded.

The woman shook her head. 'If he wants you to know, he'll tell you himself. I'll tell you this much, though. She'll not be back, and good riddance. He doesn't need her, and no more does the child—but I've said enough. Ask him—if you dare—but pick your moment. He's awful touchy about it still.'

Jamie had noticed—and she had no intention of asking him about any such thing. Besides, it was by no means certain that she'd even get the chance!

CHAPTER TWO

IT WASN'T a good night. Between the strange bed, the uncertainty about her future and Rob Buchanan's anger over her inquisitiveness, Jamie didn't sleep much.

Her room was above the front door, and so she was aware of the exact number of times Rob was called out, and how long he was gone each time.

By five-thirty, when he left again, he had been in for precisely four hours, in three stretches, since the unfortunate scene in the kitchen—this on top of an already punishing schedule and at the start of a no doubt hectic week. Jamie sighed. Why was he so determined to get rid of her? Mrs H's words came back to her. 'If ever a man needed help it's that one.' Well, it was up to her to make him accept it—at least temporarily.

Throwing off the bedclothes, she made her way to the bathroom, had a quick wash and then dressed in the colourful and pretty tracksuit she had worn the previous night. With her trainers in her hand, she crept down the silent landing and tiptoed down the stairs, letting out her breath as she closed the kitchen door behind her. She put the kettle on and made a cup of tea, and then while it cooled she started her warm-up routine. She was standing head-down with her back to the door and her hands grasping one ankle when she heard a slight noise behind her. Peering through her legs, she saw a large pair of shoes at the bottom of impossibly long legs clad in lovat-green wool trousers.

She dropped her ankle as if it were red-hot and snapped upright.

'Good morning.'

She shoved the hair off her face with both hands and turned reluctantly to face him, conscious of the flush on her cheeks and, strangely, every curve and hollow of her slender body. She tugged the tracksuit top down and tried for a smile.

'Morning. Would you like a cup of tea?'

'I haven't had a better offer all day,' he murmured. He hooked a chair with his foot and dropped wearily into it, one arm lying along the table-top with the elbow bent and his head propped on his hand.

She found another cup and filled it, then set it down beside him. His eyes were shut, and he looked absolutely exhausted. His skin was grey, the dark hair heavy on his brow in stark contrast. There were black shadows under his eyes, and his cheeks were hollowed and deeply etched. He needed a shave, and the dark stubble did nothing to improve his appearance. He looked like a convict on the run, a man at the end of his tether. She stifled the urge to pull his head against her breast and smooth away the cares, instead perching on a chair near him and watching him with steady eyes.

After a few seconds a soft snore escaped him, and she realised he was asleep, bolt upright in the chair. Poor man. Poor, exhausted, stubborn, foolish man. She reached out and touched his arm lightly, and his eyes flickered and opened slowly.

'Sorry,' he muttered gruffly, and reached almost blindly for the tea.

'Bad night,' she stated gently, and he nodded.

'Did I disturb you?'

She shook her head. 'Not really, no.'

'Just wondered. You're up awful early.'

'I was going for a run. It looks a lovely morning.'

He nodded. 'It is.' He cocked his head on one side. 'Mind if I join you? I could do with a little fresh air.'

Well, what could she say? No, I want to be on my own? Yes, by all means, but keep your rotten temper to yourself?

'That would be very nice,' she said instead, and wondered why she didn't choke on the lie. Still, it would give her a chance to be with him, and perhaps they could talk again about the practice. He couldn't deny that he needed help, and she was ready, willing and able—not to mention having a contract in her handbag, which must surely mean something?

She stirred the dregs of her tea idly while he went and changed, and the thoughts ran endlessly round in a continuous loop, always coming back to the same thing—if Rob Buchanan wouldn't let her help him, there was nothing she could do about it.

He was back quickly, and she pushed herself to her feet before she turned to look at him. Instantly, she wished she had remained seated, because he was dressed in nothing more than a pair of satin running shorts and a running vest that did nothing to hide him from her eyes, and he was hugely, overpoweringly—well, male, really, she thought with a last vestige of humour. It was just that the word *man* was suddenly redefined before her eyes, and it frankly took her breath away.

'Ready?'

'I—yes, of course.' She pushed the chair under the table, took a deep breath and followed him down the hall. He stood back to hold the door for her, and she squeezed past him, skilfully avoiding contact. 'Which way do we go?' she asked quietly.

'Up out of the village, along the glen and then back round to the coast road and home—about four miles. Is that OK?'

She nodded. Three miles was her usual run, but she hadn't done it recently because of all the confusion and packing up and—well, she just hadn't. Still, she could. 'I'll follow you,' she said, and it was the last thing she managed for some time.

He set a punishing pace, and she fell into step behind him with a feeling of dread. Was he doing it on purpose? Probably. She gritted her teeth and tucked her head down, keeping just his heels in sight. It served two purposes. One, it stopped her having to see the length of the hill they were climbing—and two, she was less aware of the powerful legs with their liberal dusting of black hair pounding like pistons ahead of her. She spared him a glance, and shook her head slightly at what she saw.

Everything about him, from the immensely powerful shoulders, through the long arms and down the powerful column of his back to the taut buttocks and massive thighs that bunched with every stride—everything shrieked MAN. Jamie didn't need that kind of distraction if she was going to have to fight with him about her job. The last thing she needed in a battle of the sexes was to be physically aware of him, or him of her, come to that. Thank God she was covered up—although as the run progressed and she heated up she wondered how long it would be before she wanted to tear off her top and let the air filter through her thin cotton T-shirt.

Too bad, she decided. Her bra was only so good, and although she was slim, she was also quite definitely a woman, and running was not calculated to make that go unnoticed. She kept the top on.

She was so busy in her thoughts that she didn't realise they had reached the top of the hill, or that Rob was waiting for her. Consequently she cannoned into him, driving her breath out with a little 'Ooof!' and bringing a blush to her already warm cheeks. He steadied her with his hands, and she felt the shock all the way down to her toes.

'You look hot,' he said unnecessarily. 'Why don't you take off the top?'

'I'll be fine,' she gasped. 'Don't want to have to carry it.'

'I'll carry it.' He held out his hand, and she hesitated only a second.

Modesty be damned, she thought as she wrenched the suffocating top off. 'I thought it would be cooler,' she said lamely.

He knotted the sleeves around his trim waist and frowned at her. 'Am I going too fast for you? You look a bit out of condition.'

'It's a few weeks since I went for a run,' she confessed. More like a few months, she corrected herself, and made a conscious effort to slow her breathing.

'All downhill now,' he said with a grin. 'Hell on the knees, but easy on the chest. Ready?'

She nodded weakly, and he set off, his long legs loping steadily down the slight incline. She kept up with him, but his stride was much longer than hers, and it wasn't easy. Once she stumbled, and his hand shot out like lightning and grabbed her arm in a vice-like grip.

'OK?'

'Yes—fine—just—thank you.'

She looked up and met his eyes, and a new respect dawned in them.

'I'll shorten my stride,' he suggested, the ghost of a smile playing around his eyes, and she stifled the retort. Playing games with her, was he?

'Don't bother,' she said, and led the way, her pace too fast but her pride flying high.

He caught up with her, shot her a grin and moved in front, deliberately racing ahead.

'Show-off,' she yelled after him, and dropped back to a more sensible speed. Her legs felt like jelly, and she wondered how much further it was. Rob was out of sight now, the bend ahead hiding him from view.

As she rounded the corner, he thrust himself away from the rock he was resting against and jogged up beside her.

'Nearly there,' he said with a smile, and she nodded briefly and concentrated on putting one foot in front of the other.

They dropped down the last section of hill to the

coast road, and then turned left, back towards the village. This stretch of road was by now familiar to Jamie, and she knew it could only be a mile or so at the most, but it seemed to stretch on forever.

Just when she felt she really couldn't go on any longer, Rob tugged her to a halt at his side. 'Let's walk,' he suggested. 'The view is breathtaking, isn't it? It never fails to move me.'

They fell into step, his long legs slowing to accommodate her shorter stride, and as they walked, he pointed things out to her.

'Salmon farm,' he said, and she squinted into the rising sun.

'Where?'

He moved round behind her, stretched out his arm and pointed. 'Look along my arm,' he instructed, and she rested her cheek against his forearm and looked.

'Oh, yes,' she said, distracted. His skin was cool and damp, covered with a fine sheen of moisture, and his body, so close behind her, smelt of soap and healthy exercise and a strange, heady fragrance that called to some long-buried primitive part of her.

She moved away.

'Rob, about what you overheard last night——'

He stiffened. 'Forget it.'

'I can't,' she said quietly. 'I didn't want you to think I was prying.'

'Weren't you?'

'No! At least, not intentionally. My father always said I leap in where angels fear to tread, but last night it didn't occur to me that there was anything to pry into. Obviously Chloe has or has had a mother, and a child of that age isn't usually brought up by the father on his own. It wasn't an unreasonable mistake to make.'

He was silent for a while, and then sighed, running his big hands through his hair. She thought he looked resigned.

'I'm sorry, I tend to over-react.'

'Tell me about her,' Jamie prompted gently.

He gave a brief snort. 'I thought Mrs Harrison already did that.'

'No.' Jamie stopped him with a hand on his arm and turned him to face her. 'She only told me she was away and wasn't coming back. Nothing else.'

'What else is there?' he said bleakly.

'There's why.'

He shot her a black look. 'Your father was right. You're an interfering baggage.'

She took a deep breath and smiled. 'Mrs H told me not to let you frighten me. I get the impression you're just a pussycat.'

He gave a wry snort of laughter, and then met her eyes candidly.

'You want to know about Jennifer? She hated it in the Highlands. We met in Edinburgh, where I trained, and when I did my GP trainee year I came out here to this practice. It was wonderful, so clean and straightforward, somehow, after the city—but within a month Jennifer had left and gone back to Edinburgh. She said she wanted a divorce, and I was tied to the practice, so I begged her to wait until the year was over and let us try again.

'She refused, and when the year was up they offered

me a job here and I took it. As soon as the second year of our separation was up, she started divorce proceedings. I took some leave and went back to Edinburgh to try and talk her out of it. At first it seemed that we might have a chance, but, when she asked me if I would consider a city practice and I said no, the most I would consider was a small rural practice just outside a city, that was it. End of reconciliation.'

His face bleak, he continued, 'Eleven months later she turned up with Chloe, eight weeks old, and said she didn't want her. I was appalled. I had no way of looking after her, so I took a few days off, shopped for baby equipment and a housekeeper, and Mrs Harrison turned up, bless her heart. She'd lost her husband, her children had left the nest and she was finding things a bit tight and a lot lonely. She's been a marvel, and without her I would have lost the only thing in the world I really care about.'

He turned away, but not before Jamie caught the bright sheen of tears in his eyes.

'So now you know,' he said a little unevenly. 'As far as Chloe's concerned, mothers don't exist.'

'And as far as you're concerned, women don't exist except in cities.' Her voice was flat, devoid of emotion. How could she fight such deep-rooted prejudice?

'That's right,' he said tersely. 'I have to get back. Do you know the way?'

She nodded, and he left her there, watching his powerful legs eating up the road as he sprinted back home. She followed slowly, her heart heavy.

How could she make him understand? The peace and tranquillity of the quiet little Scottish backwater were just what her spirit needed after the last harrowing year. Perhaps he would give her a trial? Yes, that was it, she'd persuade him to allow her to help, make herself indispensable and then he'd have no option. . .

She shook her head. It wouldn't work. He wasn't a man who allowed circumstances to dictate to him. As she let herself in the front door, she was almost resigned to putting her overnight bag back in the car and driving back to—where? Her parents' house was sold, her half-brother and his wife didn't want or need her—she had nowhere to go. No home, no job, friends who were too busy chasing the ladder of success to bother with a restless young woman who couldn't settle down. No good telling them that her soul was starved. They would only laugh.

Rob was standing in the hall with Chloe in his arms, talking on the phone as she walked in. He looked worried, and as she went up the stairs she heard him say he'd be there in fifteen minutes.

He put Chloe in the kitchen with Mrs H and bounded past Jamie on the stairs, going up three at a time. He ran into his bedroom, stripping off his vest as he went, and seconds later she heard drawers slamming.

She tapped on the open bedroom door, and he glanced up, clad only in a pair of skimpy briefs. She dragged her eyes from his body, aware that this was not the time to be distracted.

'Can I help?' she offered quietly.

He looked at her as if she were an answer to his prayers, and nodded.

'School bus overturned on the main road. Have you got a medical bag in your car?'

'Yes, of course.'

'Throw something on and bring it. I'll get some syringes and some diamorphine from the dispensary, and we'll need giving sets and some saline——'

She didn't wait to hear the familiar list.

They met in the hall a few seconds later. He stuck his head round the kitchen door, rattled off instructions to Mrs H and joined her at the Land Rover.

'Got the bag?'

She nodded.

'Come on, then.'

He drove at breakneck speed, and when they arrived she could see why. It was a scene of absolute mayhem. Terrified children clustered round each other some yards from the bus, which lay on its side at the edge of the road. As they approached, the policeman who had been first on the scene greeted them with relief.

'Most of the kids are fine—cuts and bruises, the odd fracture—one arm, a couple of fingers. A WPC is giving them some first aid and a bit of TLC. Two children still trapped inside—both still alive, but one has head injuries and probably leg injuries, and the other has abdominal injuries from the crushed seat in front of her.'

'Have their parents been informed?' Rob asked tersely.

'Doing it now. The two in the bus are apparently Stephen Watson and Trudy Douglas——'

'Trudy?' Rob's face lost its colour and he closed his eyes. 'Come on, Jamie. You come with me into the bus and we'll see if we can get them out.'

They made their way in through the smashed windscreen, past the rows of broken seats to the two children trapped near the back. There was a policewoman crouched beside them, murmuring reassuringly to Trudy. Rob, hunched up in the cramped roof of the bus, reached Trudy first.

'Hello, Trudy, love,' he said gently. 'We'll soon have you out of here. Tell me where you hurt, hen.'

She lifted wide, terrified eyes at him and gave him a trembly little smile. 'Hello, Dr Rob,' she whispered. 'I think my effluent's oozed out; I'm all wet,' she told him.

'Is it just the tummy?' he asked, and she nodded.

He quickly assessed the extent of the damage, and then turned to Jamie. 'I'm going to have to get her out to deal with her. I think I may be able to shift the seat if you can steady her—think you can manage it? It's a bit awkward.'

'I'll be fine,' she told him. 'This little boy's unconscious, but his vital signs seem fairly strong. He's trapped by the legs. I think most of the blood's from a scalp wound.'

Rob nodded. 'We'll get Trudy out first before we try and move him.'

He got a line into her arm, ran in some saline and gave her a small shot of pethidine, examining the seat while it took effect. Then he positioned Jamie under Trudy so she wouldn't fall when the seat was moved, and braced his legs against the roof and the seat behind.

'Ready?' he murmured, and winked at Trudy. Then he bunched his muscles and heaved, and the seat creaked up and eased steadily away. She slithered on to Jamie's lap with a little cry, and Jamie's arms wrapped instinctively around the brave little girl.

'All right, sweetheart, soon have you out and comfy,' she crooned reassuringly, as Rob gave the seat one last wrench and cleared the way. Then he stooped and lifted Trudy from her lap, and bore her tenderly out of the bus to lie on the grass outside.

It was immediately obvious that it was more than her dialysate that had leaked. Her school uniform was soaked with blood, and Rob looked desperately worried.

She met his eyes over Trudy's body, and could have wept for them both. So much for not getting involved with one's patients, she thought with a wry little smile.

'Where the hell is the ambulance?' he muttered. Just then they heard the siren blaring in the distance, and in seconds it came into view, slewing off at the side of the road. Immediately the crew leapt out and ran over.

'Internal injuries,' Rob said briskly. 'It isn't helped by the fact that she's on CAPD.'

The ambulanceman bent over Trudy and touched the tip of her nose. 'We know you, don't we, pet? Old friends, aren't we, Trudy? Coming for a ride?'

Jamie left the three of them and took the other ambulanceman to the bus. He produced some cutters which made short work of the seat and they soon had the little boy free. His legs were both broken below the knee, but he moaned as they moved him, a good sign that his unconsciousness wasn't too deep. Jamie got in a line and cleaned up the head wound while the ambulanceman splinted both the boy's legs and fetched a stretcher. Soon both the children were loaded into the ambulance and were away, leaving Rob and Jamie to deal with the walking wounded.

By the time the last of the children had been either sent to hospital or collected by their parents, it was ten o'clock and Rob was showing the effects of the night on call.

They drove back in silence, both preoccupied with their thoughts, and when they arrived at the house Rob led her round to the back door and up the back stairs to the landing.

'The hall will be full of patients, and neither of us is exactly inspiring to look at,' he said ruefully.

Jamie had to agree. If she looked half as bad as him. . .!

'Rob, let me help you with your surgery,' she said urgently. 'Those people have had a long wait already and they have work to get on with.'

He studied her in silence for a time, and then gave a weary nod. 'Thank you. I'll accept—for them. See you downstairs in five minutes.'

Well, she thought, progress!

She showered rapidly, washing her hair and tying it back to dry while she tugged on a skirt and jumper and slid her feet into sandals. She went down the back way and met Mrs H in the kitchen.

'Congratulations!' the housekeeper whispered. 'I knew you'd be good for him. He says you're to use the little surgery next to the office. The notes are on the desk. Away and get started, and I'll bring you a cup of coffee in a minute.'

Jamie crossed the hall, smiling at the assembled patients who looked back curiously.

'Good morning!' she said brightly, and they mumbled a ragged response. She smiled grimly to herself. They weren't giving anything away to a stranger! The surgery was small but clean and neat—lacking Rob's chaotic influence, she thought, and also his warmth. She would have to get some posters up to brighten it.

She picked up the first set of notes, walked to the door and stuck her head round. 'Mrs Ferguson? Could you come in, please?'

Mrs H brought her a cup of coffee between her third and fourth patients, and she gulped it down gratefully before carrying on. After about an hour, she found that the pile of notes had moved from one side of her desk to another, and with a sigh and a stretch she walked to the door and looked out into the empty hall. Rob's door was open, and she could hear him on the phone.

It went down with a crash, and he swore softly. She tapped on the door.

'Come in!' he barked.

She did, quirking an eyebrow at him, and he sighed and grinned ruefully.

'What do you want first—the good news or the bad news?'

She answered his smile.

'Good, of course.'

'Trudy's going to be fine. The blood was from her exit site, which must have got torn when the seat trapped her. She's a bit sore, but nothing drastic. She is, of course, back on haemodialysis until the site settles down,' he added heavily.

'And the bad?'

'Can't get a locum for at least a fortnight.'

She tried to stifle the smile, but failed. 'Why is that such bad news? You've got me.'

'Huh!' he snorted. 'Now I have, but for how long? I have to get someone permanent and reliable before the winter sets in,' he explained patiently, as if she were an idiot.

She leant over the desk and stabbed her finger into his rock-hard chest. 'I am here, and I am permanent, and I am reliable.'

He took her hand in his, and the warmth shot up her arm, stunning her.

'Jamie, be reasonable,' he pleaded.

She snatched her hand away, partly because he was irritating her, and partly because she couldn't concentrate for wondering when her arm was going to catch fire.

'I'm being perfectly reasonable,' she argued, spinning away from the desk and moving to the window. Chloe was outside, playing in the sandpit in a pair of bright pink dungarees and a clashing yellow T-shirt. She watched as the child made a sandcastle and then smashed it down with a delicious chuckle.

She was aware of Rob standing beside her, his face hard as he stared past her at his beloved daughter. She laid a hand on his arm, and felt again the warmth coursing through her veins.

'Rob, not everyone is like your wife.'

'Ex-wife,' he corrected, and shifted his eyes to hers.

'I'm sorry, Jamie, my mind's made up. I have no choice but to accept your help for a while, but you may as well start looking for another job somewhere more suitable.'

'Damn you, you insufferable, chauvinistic, pig-headed fool! I don't *want* another job! I want *this* one, and I'm damn well going to have it!'

She turned on her heel and cannoned into Mrs H, who was standing in the doorway with an approving smile on her face.

With a muttered apology she squeezed past her and fled upstairs, slamming her bedroom door and counting to ten to try and get a handle on her rage.

A few minutes later there came a tap at the door.

'Who is it?'

'An insufferable, chauvinistic, pig-headed fool. May I come in?'

Lord, she thought, did I really call him all that?

'Yes, come in.' She got off the bed and turned to face him. 'I'm sorry about the adjectives——'

'Don't be.' He gave her a lop-sided grin. 'I expect I deserve them all, and more besides. I have a proposition for you. Suppose you stay for the full two months of the trial period?'

'And will you give me a fair run? Put your preconceived notions on hold and give me a chance to prove myself?'

He grinned. 'Yes—as if you'd give me a choice!'

She sat down on the bed with a plonk, her mind whirling. Two months took them up to the end of October. The weather was starting to break up then, and hopefully he wouldn't be able to do anything about another partner until the spring—by which time. . .

'I accept,' she said quickly.

He gave her a wry grin. 'I rather thought you might. It only took Jennifer half that time to find out she hated it. It should be long enough to convince you.'

'Or you,' she said challengingly.

'Stubborn little thing, aren't you?'

She grinned. 'Oh, yes—every bit as stubborn as you, and then some, probably.'

'I doubt it,' he said with a laugh.

She raised an eyebrow. 'Don't be too sure.'

The challenge hung in the air between them.

CHAPTER THREE

JAMIE'S first and most pressing concern was accommodation. She tackled Rob about it after they had finished the evening surgery and were sitting down in the cosy little room at the end of the hall. Chloe had thrown all her toys out on to the floor and was playing happily in the toybox, the television was on quietly and Rob was motionless for the first time in twenty-four hours.

She came straight to the point and asked him outright where he suggested she should live during her 'trial' period. She found herself thinking of it in inverted commas, because she had decided she was staying. The term 'trial' was Rob's and his alone.

'I think you'd be best off here, if you're really serious about doing this properly,' he said thoughtfully. 'How else will we manage when you're on call at night—or weren't you thinking of doing nights?' He asked the question quietly and seriously, and Jamie was almost fooled. Then she caught the glimmer of challenge in those amazing eyes of his.

'Certainly I'm going to do nights,' she returned, refusing to rise to the bait. 'Unless you think a mere woman isn't to be trusted?'

He studied her for a second, his dark blue-grey eyes assessing, and then he smiled wryly. 'Of course I trust you—*medically*, I have no qualms at all. Your references were excellent, and I've had a stream of calls telling me about the nice young lady doctor and how pleasant you are!'

She smiled. 'That's because they're used to you pretending to be ferocious!' she teased.

He chuckled. 'I'm only ferocious with time-wasters who should know better—I got fairly crotchety this morning with an old boy who called me out at four because he'd been to his sister's and had a heavy meal and was plagued by indigestion! Silly old goat. I didn't need that in the middle of last night!' He sighed and stretched, and the old sofa creaked under his weight.

'Can I do tonight for you?' Jamie offered.

He shook his head wearily, but he looked seriously tempted. 'You don't know your way round yet,' he said. 'No, what I suggest is that you come with me this week when I do the calls in the day, and then you can start to take over the daytime calls until you're used to the area—another week or so. I don't mind doing the nights for a while, especially if I've got help in the day so I can rest if I need to.'

Chloe, bored with her toys, chose that moment to climb out of the toybox and run up to her father. 'Daddy!' she said imperiously, and took him by the hand. 'Come! Play Chloe!'

He let her drag him to the floor, and sat cross-legged against the wall next to the toybox while she piled bricks in his lap.

'House!' she demanded.

He built a house, and she knocked it down, and he built another, and then another, and after a while she grew bored and turned to him, scaling his big body like a tiny mountaineer, grabbing fristfuls of clothes to help her ascent. He lifted his arms up and swung her round on to his shoulders, and she sat there, her fingers buried in his hair, and jerked it.

'Come on, horsey!' she ordered, and then he was crawling round the floor, Chloe balanced on his back, giggling and shrieking and giving orders right, left and centre.

Jamie curled her feet up under her out of the way, and watched in awe as the tiny child bent the big man to her will. He was putty in her hands, she thought fondly, and her throat closed up on a lump as she watched them at play. Oh, lord, she thought, don't tell me I'm going to fall for the man!

''Gain!' Chloe squealed when he stopped, but he shook his head.

'Bedtime for you, sweetheart,' he said gently but firmly, and swung her down into his arms.

As he straightened he caught Jamie's eyes, and beneath Chloe's chubby starfish hands his craggy cheeks flushed. 'I'll just put her to bed. Could you get the phone if it rings and tell me if it's anything urgent?'

Then he was gone, his firm tread retreating along the hall and up the stairs, leaving her alone. A little while later she heard water running, and then splashing and giggling. Then all was quiet, and if she listened hard she could hear his voice, a deep and steady rumble in the distance, reading his daughter a bedtime story.

The lump in her throat grew until Jamie thought it would choke her, and she stood up abruptly, slipping her feet into her sandals and letting herself out of the French doors into the peaceful garden.

She had been here twenty-four hours—the first day

of her 'trial' period—and she wondered what her new boss had made of her. Hopefully she hadn't made any mistakes—apart from the unavoidable one of being born female! She wondered how Trudy was doing, and if Mrs McKay had been discharged from the cottage hospital with her Colles' fracture.

Tomorrow Josie Reeve, the girl with the large baby who had had the false alarm, would be going to the branch surgery twelve miles away for a routine ante-natal check. She was due to deliver in six weeks. If she was overdue and Jamie was forced to leave, she wouldn't see the baby into the world—and that seemed sad.

It all depended on Rob, and whether he could be persuaded to accept her as his partner. Jamie sighed. It seemed a big 'if' on which to base your life's plans, but she had nothing else. With her father's death and Martin's subsequent rejection—no, she wouldn't think about him tonight. It was a beautiful evening, and he wasn't worth wasting it on.

She rested her hands on the garden wall and stared out over the ruffled waters of the loch. There was a light breeze teasing at her hair, and it brought with it the crying of the gulls and the sigh of the waves against the rocky shore.

Peace, perfect peace, she thought. All she needed to make it paradise was someone to share it with—someone like-minded and intelligent, blessed with a quick wit and a ready laugh, a gentle touch and the steadiness of a rock. An image thrust itself insistently into her mind, and she dismissed it with a rueful laugh, turning back towards the house—and Rob.

As if her lonely imagination had conjured him out of thin air, he stood there, one hand against the door frame, regarding her steadily.

'Homesick?'

'Oh, no—never that! Anyway, I have no home any more. This is it—the only home I have.' With a light laugh, she waved a hand at her surroundings.

The sudden surge of loneliness tugged at her shoulders and they drooped wearily, sick of bearing the burden of responsibility alone. But it was over now, her father was at rest, her childhood home sold, emptied, small pieces of it packed away, like a Pandora's box of memories, stored in a friend's attic. And Martin—Martin had lost interest as soon as the reality of her father's mortgage had reduced his hopes of an advantageous marriage to dust.

She wasn't aware that Rob had moved until his hand cupped her cheek and brushed away the tears.

A sob caught in her throat, and he gathered her against his hard chest and murmured wordlessly to her as if she were Chloe. When the tears had dried to the occasional hiccupping sob, he led her to a stone seat set in the rose garden at the the end and handed her his handkerchief.

'Want to talk about it?' he said gently. She shook her head. She had made enough of a fool of herself without adding to it.

'I'm just tired,' she said lamely, and he laughed, a short, harsh chuckle.

'Is that all?' he said with wry humour. 'Sometimes I think I could lie down and die from being just tired.

Perhaps I'll cry all over you—will it make me feel better?'

She gave him a wobbly grin. 'No, it'll make you feel an absolute fool,' she said honestly.

His mouth lifed in a sympathetic smile. 'Don't. You've had a couple of long days run into each other, and I get the feeling that's the least of your worries. Why don't you catch an early night so you're ready to start work tomorrow? I want you to come to the branch surgery with me and meet the patients, see how we do things. OK? I'll wake you at seven.'

He walked her to the bottom of the stairs, and watched her silently as she climbed them, still slightly stiff from their run. When she reached the top she turned back and looked down at him. He looked wonderful—big and craggy and solid and dependable—a rock, an anchor in life's tempestuous seas. Her lips curved in a smile.

'Thank you, Rob,' she said softly.

He stared back at her without a word, and a sudden flare of hunger lit his eyes. Her heart quickening, she turned away and walked the last few steps to her room.

As she closed the door, he spoke softly.

'Sleep tight, princess.'

At least, she thought that was what he said, but the whisper that curled round the stairs and floated down the corridor faded softly into the night. Perhaps it was just wishful thinking.

The branch surgery was held in the village hall of Glenlivie, in a little back room next to the kitchen.

Rob's huge body dwarfed it, and she felt his nearness so acutely that she could hardly breathe.

Not that she had time, because the waiting-room was packed and there were visits to make after surgery.

The third patient was Josie Reeve, and, while Rob examined her and checked her weight and blood-pressure, Jamie tested the urine sample and found it normal. He arranged for her to have a scan, and when she left the room, Rob caught Jamie's eye and frowned.

'What's wrong?'

'I don't think her dates are right. She seems too big for thirty-four weeks. That breech is well up under her ribs, and the head's fairly well down.'

'If she goes to term, will she be able to deliver normally?'

Rob shrugged. 'Possibly. It'll be a close-run thing. Fortunately it'll all be over before the winter sets in, because there's no way I'd consider letting her deliver at home. It'll be easier to tell once the baby's rotated rather than lying occipito-posterior, if it does turn, but I reckon they'll let her have a trial and then maybe do a section if necessary.'

He strode round the desk, opened the door and called in the next patient.

Feeling like a fifth wheel, Jamie did what little she could, watched how he worked and tried not to stare at him when he wasn't looking.

Then the surgery was over, they were back in the Land Rover and heading out towards Mrs McKay's house.

She was waiting at the door by the time they got out of the car, her face wreathed in smiles. 'Dr Buchanan!

And Dr Cameron too—what a pleasant surprise! Can I get you a cup of tea? Come away in!'

He grinned and cupped her soft, wrinkled cheek in his huge palm. His thumb traced the shadows under her eyes, and his smile softened.

'That would be lovely, but we're a bit pushed for time. How about letting Dr Cameron make the tea while I have a wee look at you, my love?'

He gently engineered her acquiescence, and Jamie found herself in the tiny kitchen boiling the kettle to the sound of his deep voice and soft laughter.

He's flirting with her, she thought in surprise, and smiled. He really was a nice man. They didn't have time to stop, but she guessed that the old widow had few visitors, and, with her wrist in plaster so that she couldn't sew, time must hang heavily on her hands. Staying to share a cup of tea with her was all part of the treatment.

The shriek of the kettle on the hob brought her back down to earth, and as she scalded the tea leaves Rob appeared at her elbow.

'Biscuits on the top shelf,' he murmured, reaching past her as she turned, and his large, warm hand settled gently against her breast.

They froze in shock for a moment, their eyes enmeshed, but then he snatched his hand away, hot colour mounting his cheeks. 'Sorry,' he mumbled, and, grabbing the biscuit tin, he thrust it at her. 'Take the tea through; I'll bring in some coal for the fire.'

Jamie could hardly stand, her legs felt so bereft of strength. Just a brief touch—an accidental brushing, and her body felt more alive than it had ever felt in her life.

He snatched up the coal bucket and slammed out of the back door, and Jamie sagged back against the stove. Dear God! Her heart raced and crashed, and deep inside something previously untouched awoke and clamoured for recognition.

With trembling hands she laid the little tray, set out a few biscuits and took the tea through to the little sitting-room.

'Here we are,' she said brightly, and set it down on the little table. 'Shall I pour?'

Mrs McKay was full of her stay in hospital, and, despite her protests about going, Jamie sensed that the company had done her good. She put in the odd comment, but her companion carried the conversation cheerfully, giving Jamie time to recover her composure.

By the time Rob came back into the room, she was sitting with Mrs McKay poring over family photos, and Rob took his tea and sat on the other side of the fire, staring broodingly into the flames.

'Where are all your family, Mrs McKay?' Jamie asked.

'Och, away now. My sister's at Fort William, but she lives in a tiny wee flat so there's no room for me to stay, and she won't come here, so I don't get to see her very often. My daughter Jane's in Edinburgh, married to a teacher—that's her, with Bill—and my son Gordon's on the rigs at Aberdeen. His wife and I don't get on too well—she says I'm a stubborn old fool.'

'So you are, but you're entitled to be,' Rob said with

a smile, and they exchanged a look of mutual affection. Then he put down his cup, straightened as far as he could under the low ceiling and stuffed his big hands into his pockets.

'You take care now. I'll come and see you again next week, but you're to call if you need me in the meantime. I've chopped you some kindling, and I'll send Mrs Harrison over with some groceries later in the week, to save you going out. You can pay her when she comes. Now you know what to do—keep it up, keep it dry and tell me if it hurts or swells or your fingers go a funny colour. OK?'

'Aye, Doctor. I'll see you next week. Bless you.'

She stood up and patted his arm, her tiny shrivelled hand so frail against the corded sinews of his powerful forearm, and he covered the little hand with his and gave it a gentle squeeze before releasing her with a smile.

'She adores you,' Jamie said as they set off again.

He grinned. 'It's mutual. She's the toughest old bird in the world, but her body can't keep up with her determination any more. I keep trying to get her to move into something more sensible, but she won't go. Her children were born there, her husband died there, and she won't leave until they carry her out in a box.'

'How sad,' Jamie said quietly, and his hand came out and found hers, his long fingers wrapping round her hand and squeezing it gently. She felt reassurance flow from him, and knew the comfort Mrs McKay had felt. She thought again of how his hand had brushed against her breast in the kitchen, and wondered how it would feel to be his wife, to know the power and tenderness of his hands on her body——

'She's content. She'll never be happy again, but she's content. There's a lot to be said for it.'

He removed his hand, and Jamie glanced at him, stunned by the raw note of defeat in his voice. His expressive face was touched with a deep sadness, and Jamie had to quell an impulsive urge to hug him. Instead she turned and stared out of the window, giving him privacy while he chased out whatever demon had possessed him.

Her mouth, however, was less considerate, as her thoughts led on from the trigger of his touch. A surge of rage and jealousy gripped her at the thought of the woman who had had him and then left him, and she was appalled to find herself asking him if he was still in love with his wife.

'God, no! After the way she dumped Chloe on me, neither knowing nor caring if I could look after her? She hasn't contacted me since that day, I don't even know where she lives, and she hasn't sent Chloe so much as a birthday card or a Christmas card since. No, I don't love her. I can hardly believe that I ever did.'

Oh, you did, Jamie thought, or you wouldn't be so bitter now. She wondered often how she could have loved Martin, but she must have done, or she wouldn't have hurt the way she did when he walked out on her.

'Will you marry again?' she persisted, appalled at her temerity but holding her breath for the answer.

'Never!' he said vehemently, his voice harsh. 'I thought my world had come to an end when Jennifer walked out on me. I really didn't believe she meant it when she said she couldn't tolerate living in the country. I thought, foolishly, that if a man and woman loved each other they would do anything to be together.'

'They will, if the love is strong enough,' Jamie protested, but his derisive glance cut her off.

'It's never strong enough if everything else doesn't fall into place. I used to think she would come back, that our love would be enough. I was naïve and deluded, but not any more. No one's going to live out here with me, and I wouldn't expect them to. Anyway, I don't need it. I know now that there are more important things, like providing a secure future for my daughter, and she's more important to me than searching for some mythical romantic ideal. I don't intend to let my happiness or hers depend on the selfish whim of some feckless woman. Besides, I know more about myself now than I did. I know I'm no good at compromise. I couldn't live in a town, and I wouldn't ask a woman to live in the country.'

'You could always marry a local girl,' she suggested.

He snorted. 'All the girls with brains have gone, and the ones left behind are either too stupid to escape or married to local lads, like Josie Reeve. No, I know what I want from a woman, and I know what I'm likely to get as long as I live here. The gulf's too wide. You'll find that soon enough. There's precious little in the way of entertainment, very few professional people and the ones there are are married. Patients, of course, are out of the question, and that leaves nobody in a fifteen-mile radius.'

'That won't worry me,' she said quietly. 'I'm not here looking for a husband.'

He shot her a quick look. 'Had your fingers burnt too?'

She looked away from his searching eyes. 'You could say that.'

'Then you understand,' he said flatly.

Oh, yes, she understood—all except one thing. Why on earth, after all that had happened and she had sworn never again—after all that, why was she so attracted to Rob Buchanan?

They finished the visits and headed back to Glencorran in time for a late lunch. Then there were more local visits, and all too soon it was time for evening surgery.

'Let me take it while you have a rest,' Jamie suggested. 'Take Chloe for a walk, or go and sit in the garden or something.'

He eyed her doubtfully. 'Will you manage?'

'Of course I'll manage! Good grief, Rob, do me a favour!'

He grinned sheepishly. 'Sorry. Well, if you're sure, I wouldn't mind running in to Fort William to see Trudy and one or two other patients. Could you hold the fort for three hours?'

'Sure. Mrs H will help me if I get totally bogged down—she can always open a soup kitchen for them while they wait!'

He laughed. A deep, rich laugh that softened his craggy face and knocked years off him, and then he bounded up the stairs three at a time, whistling cheerfully.

Smiling to herself, Jamie found the surgery list and set about tracking down the notes.

By the time he got back at nine she had finished surgery and was sitting down at the desk in the office, having a go at the mountains of paperwork. He found her there behind a huge pile of forms, a pencil stabbed into her hair and a distracted expression on her face.

'You should be claiming all this lot,' she said briskly. 'You're throwing away income, you know.'

He laughed ruefully. 'I haven't had time to think about income.'

'What about getting a secretary?'

'We had one.'

'And?'

He shrugged. 'She left to have a baby. I can't get a replacement.'

'Has she had it yet?'

He nodded. 'Yes. He's three months old. Why?'

'Just wondered. Would she like to come back?'

'What about the baby?'

Jamie gave him a considering look. 'How about Mrs Harrison? Would she mind babysitting him for a few hours a week? That's all it would take if we were well organised.'

He hitched one hip on to the desk and looked down at her. 'I'll ask Mrs H. In the meantime, have you had anything to eat?'

She pushed the chair away from the desk and tilted her head back to look up at him. 'No, and I'm starving. I thought I'd wait and see if you'd eaten, and throw something together for us both. Chloe's in bed, and Mrs H has gone up to her room to watch the television.'

'Sounds good. I'll be with you in a minute when I've kissed Chloe goodnight.'

He straightened up and headed for the door, and Jamie followed him.

By the time he came back downstairs, she had whipped up some eggs and had a heavy pan on the stove with some left-over ham and vegetables sizzling gently in butter.

'Real low-cholestrol stuff, this,' she said with a grin.

He peered over her shoulder. 'Smells great. Shall I throw a salad together?'

'Would you? The salad things are in the fridge—oh, you know!' She laughed self-consciously. 'Sorry, I forgot this is your house.'

'Don't worry about it—sometimes I forget, too. I've only been here for six months, since my senior partner died and the practice came up for sale.'

'Was it his?'

Rob nodded. 'Uh-huh. I think there was a bit of price-rigging with the executors because they knew I was after it—makes sense, not having to relocate the practice. In fact the little sitting-room at the back would make an ideal waiting-room if I had time to sort out the other room round the side—it's much bigger and would make a lovely play-room for Chloe, but I just don't get any time to tackle it.'

'Maybe you will, now I'm here.'

He studied her in silence. 'Maybe. I wonder how long you'll last?'

'Forever, given the chance,' she returned, and met his gaze unflinchingly.

'No way. Your hormones will start acting up and

you'll want the bright lights and the parties and the nightlife——'

'Do you?'

His gaze didn't falter. 'Sometimes—not the bright lights or the parties, but the rest—sometimes.'

'We could always have an affair,' she heard herself say, and then swallowed as he speared her with his eyes.

For endless minutes he held her trapped in the beam of desire that darkened his eyes to midnight, then he laughed and turned away, shattering the tension.

'Did you mean to say that?' he asked, and his voice sounded oddly strained.

'No—no, I don't think I did,' she mumbled.

'Pity. It would have been a very convenient arrangement. No strings, you going in two months——'

'I'm not going, Rob,' she said quietly.

His mouth tightened to a grim line. 'We'll see.'

His gaze flicked behind her, then returned, his humour restored. 'Tell me something.'

She swallowed. What now? 'Yes?'

'Did you mean to burn the omelettes?'

CHAPTER FOUR

For the next two days Jamie accompanied Rob almost everywhere, and it gradually dawned on her what he had been dealing with in the time since his senior partner had died. The locums who had filled the gap until recently had had no more knowledge of the area than her, and so the burden of the visits must have still fallen heavily on Rob.

But for the past three weeks he had been managing totally single-handed, and it was a punishing schedule that would have had most men on their knees.

As it was, by the end of Thursday Rob was almost literally asleep on his feet and Jamie insisted that he allow her to take the night calls.

His acquiescence was a measure of his exhaustion. He merely nodded, thanked her abuptly, and almost crawled up the stairs to bed.

As things turned out it was a quiet night, and she had no calamities to report to him in the morning, much to their mutual relief.

He looked better, although Jamie privately thought that only a month flat on his back in the tropics could put the colour back in his cheeks.

'I'll do the weekend,' she said firmly, and he opened his mouth to argue and yawned prodigiously instead.

'You were saying?' she said with a smile, and he shook his head, laughing ruefully.

'You win—thank you. I might take the wee beastie out to the beach for the day. There's a little cove up near here, and if the weather's nice we can paddle in the sea and play in the rockpools.'

'Sounds lovely,' Jamie said, and thought wistfully that it would be fun to go with them, and take a picnic lunch to eat on the rocks overlooking the sea. He could put the baby on his shoulders and they could go for a walk along the headland, towards the lighthouse——

'Is there a lighthouse?' she asked.

He nodded. 'At the end, yes. It's about three miles away by road, but you can walk to it round the headland. Why?'

She shrugged. Now she was picking images out of his mind! 'No reason. I was just trying to picture it.'

'Pity you can't come, but one of us has to be on duty.'

That had already occurred to Jamie, and she had found herself quite ridiculously dismayed at the thought that they would never be able to take an evening off and go out knowing that they would be undisturbed. Now she brushed aside his concern and went to get ready for morning surgery. Rob was to go to Glenlivie and do the branch surgery and outlying visits, while she was to see their local patients and do the visits closer to home. She also vowed to get in more time in the office, which reminded her. . .

She found him in the dispensary, assembling the drugs he was most likely to need and making up the repeat prescriptions.

'Rob? Did you ask Mrs Harrison about minding the secretary's baby?'

He lifted his head and looked at her as if she had spoken in Russian.

'We talked about it the other day—remember?'

He shook his head. 'No, I haven't—I'm sorry, I forgot.'

She glanced around at the chaos and smiled to herself. How could he possisbly forget with this tip as a constant reminder?

'Shall I sound her out?'

He screwed the lid back on a jar and eyed her thoughtfully, then shook his head. 'No, let me. She might think there's a conflict of interests if it comes from you.'

She didn't see him again until late that day, when he got back from Glenlivie, and by then the problem was solved.

'Mrs H thinks getting Jackie back is a wonderful idea, and Jackie agrees, so she's coming in on Monday for a couple of hours initially until we work something out,' Jamie told him.

Afterwards she told herself she should have expected the reaction, but at the time all she could think of was how unreasonable he was being.

'How dare you discuss matters of duties and staffing with my employees?' he roared. 'I thought we'd agreed that I should speak to Mrs Harrison? What right do you think you have to tackle them on the subject? Damn it, Dr Cameron, mind your own bloody business, would you? This is my practice—you are here on sufferance——'

'I thought I was here on trial,' she commented drily, and he glared at her.

'—on sufferance,' he repeated, 'and I do not intend to have my relationship with my other staff jeopardised because you can't keep your damn mouth shut!'

She shut it then—shut it so hard she nearly cracked her teeth—and turned on her heel and left, slamming the door angrily behind her and stalking off, blinking the tears of rage from her eyes so hard that she didn't see Mrs H open the door behind her and slip quietly through it.

She was in her room hurling things into her suitcase when Rob walked in unannounced and came and stood beside her, his hands in his pockets, his face bleak.

'Why didn't you tell me Jackie had brought the babe in for his injection and that she and Mrs H had already discussed it and mentioned it to you? You just stood there and let me rant on at you and insult you.'

She paused with a handful of undies and gave him a withering look. 'What was I supposed to do—tell you to shut up?'

He gave a grim little laugh. 'It wouldn't be the first time.'

She looked away, not ready to be wooed by his humble act.

'You could have believed in me. You didn't need to jump to the wrong conclusion straight away, you know. I said I would leave it up to you—why couldn't you trust me?'

He shook his head in disbelief. 'You damned yourself out of your own mouth, Jamie! You could have put it better, you know. It wouldn't have taken any longer to tell me that Jackie had come in and she and Mrs H had talked about her returning to work and what a coincidence, instead of which you launch straight in with what sounded like a self-administered pat on the back for your organisational ability——'

'Rubbish. You just didn't let me finish——'

'You'd said enough——'

'You're doing it again! Damn it, don't interrupt!'

She glared at him in silence for several seconds, seconds in which she became aware that her chest was heaving with indignation and Rob's eyes were transfixed by the sight of her breasts straining against the fine cotton lawn of her blouse. A slow flush ran up her neck into her cheeks, and he lifted his laughing eyes to hers.

'Finished?' he said softly, and she threw down the silk and lace teddy she was holding and plonked on to the bed, utterly deflated.

He reached out and picked up the battered scrap of ivory silk, his thumb tracing soft circles on it. It slithered over his fingers and dangled by a slender strap, and he held it up and looked at it, then at her. She blushed fire-engine red and lunged for it.

'Such decadence,' he murmured, and dangled it in front of her.

She snatched it from his hand and screwed it into a ball.

'Gently,' he tutted, and his mouth quirked into a grin. 'Don't destroy it before I've seen you in it!'

'You will never see me in it!' she vowed.

'Pity!'

She glared at him. 'You keep saying that!'

He turned away, his face bleak again. 'Perhaps I mean it,' he said quietly.

She had a sudden and irrational urge to cry.

'What are you doing here, Rob?'

His vast shoulders shrugged, and then seemed to sag. 'Trying to apologise. I'm not very good at it.'

'Lack of practice, I expect,' Jamie said with a touch of asperity, and then felt guilty.

'You're quite right. It's not a positon I find myself in often.'

'Once I thought I was wrong, but I was mistaken,' Jamie muttered under her breath.

He flushed, and then his mouth softened into a wry grin. 'I am sorry. Please stay.'

Her heart leapt. He really wants me here, she thought, and then he went on, 'I've told Chloe I've got the weekend off—she'll be so disappointed if I have to work.'

Jamie's heart sank. 'Of course I'll stay—for Chloe, and for the weekend.'

'Only the weekend?' he asked, his voice flat, his face curiously shuttered. She stared at him, as if trying to force an answer from his guarded features, and he looked away.

'That depends,' she said.

'On what?'

'On you. On why you want me to stay, and how you treat me, and whether you feel you can trust me and my integrity without jumping to conclusions all the time.'

He sighed and ran his hand through his hair. 'I've apologised—what more do you want, for God's sake?'

She relented then, because he sounded so tired and confused and defeated—not just by her, but by life itself, and she was nothing if not a softie. And anyway, she wanted the job more than she had ever wanted anything in her life.

Not stopping to work out why, she crossed over to him and laid her hand on his shoulder.

'OK, I'll stay.'

He turned slowly towards her, his face taut, and then it relaxed into a slight smile of relief.

'Thank you. I don't really deserve you, do I?'

She grinned. 'Probably not, but if I have my way you'll be stuck with me.'

She went up on tiptoe and kissed his cheek, and his arms went round her to steady her, his warm hands resting lightly on her back.

She sank back on to her heels, suddenly aware of the nearness of his body and the hunger that leapt to life in her at his touch.

Slowly, very slowly, his hands slid up into her hair and tilted her head as his mouth came down across hers, his lips warm and firm, brushing lightly over hers and then settling gently into place.

Her arms came up of their own accord and circled his waist, easing her body closer to his, and with a muffled groan he deepened the kiss, dragging her down in a widening spiral until she felt she was spinning out of control. She was aware of the sharp, sweet taste of his mouth, the warmth of his skin under her hands, the taut press of her breasts against his rock-hard chest. Their hearts were beating together, racing faster with every passing moment.

At last he lifted his head and Jamie whimpered, her

hands blindly reaching for him and pulling his head down to her own, claiming his mouth again.

'No!' he murmured raggedly, easing away from her, and with a desperate little cry she let him go. As she did so, shame washed over her, leaving her weak and shaken—or was that the kiss?

Mortified by her wanton reaction, she didn't know or care.

'I'm sorry,' she blurted unhappily, 'I didn't mean—oh, lord—Rob, I—damn it!'

She turned away, hot tears of shame and confusion scalding her cheeks as she battled with her fraught emotions. No one had ever kissed her like that—ever! Not even Martin in his most passionate moments had reached into her soul and shaken its foundations, but Rob. . .! One single, fairly chaste kiss and she was ready to wrench her clothes off and fling herself at his feet—oh, my God, she thought, what if he hadn't stopped me?

She was so busy wallowing in misery and shame that she didn't hear his footsteps until he was right behind her. Hugging her arms around her waist, she bowed her head and swallowed.

'I'm sorry, Rob. I didn't mean to throw myself at you.'

He didn't touch her, for which she was profoundly grateful, but his words reached out and wrapped round her, comforting her just the same.

'Jamie, don't. One of us had to have the sense to put on the brakes. Perhaps I've got more to lose than you. Believe me, I didn't want to stop, but I know I can't have it all, and I can't afford to drive you away at the moment. I need you as a friend and a colleague far more than I need you as a lover. Anyway,' he added bitterly, 'at least this way perhaps I won't hate myself when you leave. Forgive me?'

He touched her then, one hand resting lightly on her shoulder, the knuckles of the other hand brushing lightly against the exposed nape of her neck, and she lifted her hand and covered his where it lay across her collarbone, warm and strong and vital, and offered in friendship. Beneath her fingers she could feel the steady beat of his pulse, and his warm breath teased her hair.

She would take what he offered, because she didn't have a choice, but she was under no illusions. Friendship was a tepid consolation prize after the taste of paradise she had been offered in his arms.

'There's nothing to forgive,' she whispered, and his fingers tightened comfortingly on her shoulder.

In the distance the phone rang, and they heard Mrs Harrison's quick tread in the hall beneath Jamie's room.

Rob eased away from her, his expressive eyes twin pools of regret and determination, and Jamie conjured a smile for him.

'Duty calls, I guess,' she said as sanely as she could manage, and slipped past him to the top of the stairs. Mrs Harrison was just coming up.

'Call, my dear,' she said, scanning Jamie's face anxiously. 'Will you take it, or Dr Buchanan?'

'I'll take it—I'm on this weekend.'

Mrs Harrison's face lit up. 'Well, praise the lord,'

she said with a smile. 'So shall I pack to go to my sister's for the weekend?'

'I think I've persuaded her to forgive me this time, Mrs H,' Rob's voice rumbled from behind Jamie.

'Aye, well there are some folks as take naturally to humility, and with others it comes a bit harder. You'll just have to work on it, Dr Buchanan,' Mrs H said with a wink at Jamie. 'I dare say you'll get plenty of practice.'

Rob groaned and Jamie gave an unladylike snort of laughter. 'I wouldn't like to push my luck, Mrs H,' she said with a chuckle. 'I think I'll quit while I'm winning.'

And with that she picked up the phone message and the notes, and left the house, her thoughts very much with the man she had left at the top of the stairs, and the coming weekend alone with him.

Saturday dawned bright and clear and gorgeous, with the promise of heat later in the day. Jamie knew this because she was on her way back from a call as the sun crawled over the horizon and bathed the hills in gold. She stopped the car by the loch and got out, drawing a deep breath of fresh, salt-laden air. The loch ran slightly north of west for a while and then turned south, running out into the sea around the fold in the hills. From where she stood she couldn't see the sea, but she could smell it, and hear the gulls and the fishing boats in the peaceful stillness of the early morning.

It had been a quiet night, one call at eleven and then nothing until this call at four-thirty, an elderly man with a heart attack. She had admitted him to the hospital in Fort William and was now on her way home. It was too late to go back to bed, and too early to be up, and as she drove back to Glencorran she wondered what time Rob would be up.

She had been very conscious last night that Mrs Harrison was away and that they were alone, but he had behaved with absolute circumspection and left her severely alone. The part of her that was disappointed she dismissed as a hussy, but the vast majority was relieved. Even so, she was looking forward to seeing him this morning in a masochistic sort of way.

The house was in silence as she went in, and she made herself a cup of tea and went into the little sitting-room at the back. After a while she became aware of thumps and bangs and childish chatter overhead, and realised that Chloe must be awake. It was still only half-past six, and Jamie wanted Rob to sleep on undisturbed as long as possible, so she made her way quietly past his door to the room in the corner where Chloe slept.

The baby was standing in her cot lobbing toys out on to the floor, and she beamed at Jamie.

''Lo!' she piped.

'Hello, sweetheart. Want a drink?' Jamie asked softly.

'Dink!' Chloe echoed, and held up her arms. Jamie lifted her out of the cot and wrinkled her nose.

'Let's do your nappy, shall we?'

She was not exactly an expert, but she wasn't a complete novice either, and between them they managed the exercise without too much problem. Jamie dressed her in a soft velour tracksuit and carried her downstairs into the kitchen. She had watched this routine before and found the juice without difficulty, handing the bottle to Chloe and letting her drink at her own pace.

'Bik!' she demanded, and Jamie gave her a rusk in her other hand. Thus satisfied, the baby was quite happy to sit on the floor in the sitting-room and chatter to herself while Jamie drank her tea.

Peace, perfect peace, Jamie thought, but it didn't last long.

'Play!' Chloe demanded.

'Bossy little thing, aren't you?' Jamie said with a smile. 'Play *please*.'

'P'ease,' Chloe said dutifully, and then giggled delightedly when Jamie got down on the floor with her and tickled her.

They were tumbling round together like puppies when Jamie rolled against something hard and yelped. Looking up, she saw about two miles of hard, hairy legs topped by a scowl. She struggled into a sitting position and grinned sheepishly.

'Sorry, we were having a game.'

'So I see,' he said shortly. 'Why didn't you wake me? I don't expect you to look after Chloe——'

'I know that! I was up anyway, and it seemed a shame to disturb you. We've been having fun, haven't we, sweetheart?'

Chloe ignored her, scrambling to her feet and waddling over to Rob. His hands were plunged into the pockets of his short towelling robe, and the neck fell open in a deep V that revealed a mass of soft, dark hair like a cloud that smothered his chest and arrowed down his flat stomach to his waist. He looked totally forbidding and unbelievably desirable

Jamie felt a rush of heat and dropped her eyes, trying to ignore the effect he was having on her. He obviously slept naked, and had woken to Chloe's voice and flung on the robe. Frankly he might as well not have bothered, because her hyperactive imagination filled in the rest and she was humiliatingly aware of every plane and hollow of his large frame.

He stooped and picked up his daughter, hitching her on to one lean hip, and Chloe buried her hands in the soft hair on his chest and tugged.

'Ow,' he mumbled, and gently disentangled her fingers. 'Want a drink?'

'She's had one, and a rusk. I changed her nappy——'

'Damn it, Jamie, that isn't your job!'

She was startled by his vehemence and the sudden blazing anger in his dark blue-grey eyes, and stepped back a pace. 'I—I didn't mind, Rob. It needed doing, and you were——'

'You could have woken me,' he said accusingly. 'Don't use my daughter to get to me, Jamie. I won't allow you to worm your way into her affections and then dump her and flit off!'

She gazed at him in disbelief for a moment, and then gave a short, bitter laugh. 'You're mad. Do you know that? Crazy. That wife of yours has driven you round the bend!'

'Leave her out of this!' he snarled.

'Why should I? You aren't! You're expecting me to act exactly like her, and you're treating me accordingly!

Yesterday you apologised for jumping to conclusions, and now today you're doing it again! Well, forget it! You told me you wanted a colleague and a friend more than you wanted a lover—well let me tell you something, buster—I'm not the slightest bit surprised that you can't get any of them!'

'I could have had you,' he said quietly, and the words fell between them, humming in the tension.

'That's ungentlemanly!' she protested breathlessly when she could speak, and his mouth quirked into a derisive smile.

'Forgive me. I didn't know you still expected me to behave like a gentleman!' he spat back.

They stared at each other for a long time, the silence broken finally by Chloe.

'Daddy?' she asked uncertainly, and he turned his head and looked in astonishment at the object of their disagreement.

'Hello, darling,' he said gently.

'No shouting!' she told him, putting her chubby hand over his mouth, and he kissed her fingers one by one and hugged her to his side.

'No shouting,' he agreed.

'Sorry.'

He frowned in puzzlement, and she poined at Jamie. 'Sorry! Tell Jamie!'

He met Jamie's eyes again, and sighed with regret. 'I'm sorry. I apologise. I didn't mean to say any of that. It's just that she's mine, and I love her, and—oh, damn, I wouldn't expect you to understand!'

Jamie let her face soften into a smile. 'But I do,' she

told him gently. 'I understand exactly, and I would never do what you accused me of.'

'Not on purpose, perhaps.'

'I'm not going, Rob. I won't let her down because I'm not going—not unless you drive me out.'

'You may leave me no choice,' he said heavily.

Their eyes locked for a second, then he spun on his heel and left the room. She heard him climbing the stairs with Chloe, chatting to her about the beach and what she was going to wear, and it was suddenly all too much.

Jamie dropped into the armchair in the corner, pulled her feet up underneath her and cried her eyes out.

CHAPTER FIVE

JAMIE was called out shortly after seven-thirty, and by the time she got back at eight-fifteen Rob was ready to go.

'Can you manage?' he asked her tersely, and she gave him a miserable glare.

'Do you care?' she bit back.

'Women!' he muttered, and she carried on past him into the office. He followed her, a map in his hand. 'We'll be here,' he said, plonking the map down in front of her. 'If you run into difficulties, come and get me.'

'I won't,' she said shortly, and he snapped the map shut and stalked out, collecting Chloe on the way. Seconds later the Land Rover roared into life and she was alone.

'Insufferable pig!' she yelled into the silent house.

Picking up the surgery list, she quickly found all the notes for the morning surgery, answered the phone and booked in two more patients, arranged to visit three others as soon as surgery was finished and opened the front door at five to nine.

It was only as she dealt with the last patient that she realised she hadn't had any breakfast, so she grabbed a sandwich from the kitchen and made her way to her first visit, munching on the way.

It was a busy morning. There were two more calls

on the answer-phone when she got in, one of whom was Mrs Douglas, Trudy's mother.

Aware of the fact that the woman was alone, Jamie went to see her first and was immediately concerned. She was pale and sweating, and had had severe low abdominal pain during the night. Jamie took her temperature and found it up to thirty-nine, and her blood-pressure was down. It was possible that the stress of Trudy's accident had triggered a relapse, but at the very least she was suffering from a urinary infection and could slide very quickly downhill if neglected.

Jamie phoned the hospital in Fort William and arranged for her admission, and while they waited for the ambulance she tidied Mrs Douglas up and packed a case for her.

'I'll make sure Dr Buchanan goes to visit Trudy and tells her that you're all right,' Jamie assured her, and then handed her over to the ambulance crew when they arrived.

Her next call was a routine reassurance job, a toddler with a virus who was flushed and feverish, off his food and generally unwell.

'Keep him quiet, give him plenty to drink and let him rest,' she advised, and then made her way back to Glencorran.

After that there was a lull, and she made herself a cup of tea and took it into the garden, sitting on the old sun-lounger in the sun near the open window so she could hear the phone. The bees were buzzing in the flowers, and in the distance a dog barked. Occasionally a car went past, but all in all it was very peaceful, and Jamie quickly fell asleep.

She woke up to an awareness of being watched, and opened her eyes, unsurprised to find Rob sitting near her on another chair, studying her thoughtfully. He was distractingly dressed in a pair of cut-off jeans and a T-shirt, stretched taut across his deep chest, and his lean, hairy knees jutted temptingly towards her.

She struggled upright, fighting with the chair's reclining mechanism, and tugged her skirt down over her knees. 'You're back early,' she said breathlessly, and pushed her hair back off her face.

'Chloe was worn out. She fell asleep in the car on the way home, and I've put her in her cot. How's it been?'

She was torn between telling him to mind his own business and sharing her concern for his patients. Professional integrity and her easygoing nature won, and she poured out her worries over Mrs Douglas.

'As if she didn't have enough on her plate,' Jamie concluded, and Rob nodded.

'Probably why, of course. Poor woman. I wonder how much longer she'll be able to look after herself and Trudy?'

Jamie had been wondering the same thing. 'What will happen to Trudy when she can't?' she asked him. 'Does she have anyone to turn to?'

He shrugged. 'Only me. The last time her mother was ill she stayed here for three weeks.'

'Here?'

He glared at her, obviously conscious of his unprofessional lapse. 'What's wrong with that?'

'Nothing,' she said quickly. 'It's just—I thought

doctors were always encouraged not to get too involved——'

He grunted. 'It doesn't always work, though. If I hadn't had her, who would have done? Who can deal with a child on CAPD better than a doctor? It just made sense, that's all.'

'I'm not criticising, Rob, I was just curious,' she said gently. 'What will happen this time? Will she come back again? And again? What about when her mother dies? Will she come to you for ever? Will the authorities let her? You aren't married, after all, and she's a girl.'

He scowled at her. 'I know that, but it may not happen anyway before she's grown up. Besides, I have Mrs H—what more could they want?'

'A wife?'

He snorted. 'You volunteering?'

She stifled a smile. 'Are you asking?'

'Hell, no!'

The smile broke free. 'I thought not. No, Rob, I wasn't volunteering, just talking through a difficult situation with you.'

He smiled slowly, reluctantly, and then laughed softly. 'God, you get me so wound up. Perhaps we ought to go to bed and get the hormones out of the way so that we can concentrate.'

'I don't think so,' she said drily, 'and don't say "Pity" or I'll clonk you one.'

He laughed again and stretched out on the sun-lounger, one arm flung up over his eyes and sighing with contentment.

'Love a cup of tea,' he murmured, cracking one eye open and peering at her under his arm.

'Well, now, you're just lucky because I was going in to put the kettle on,' she said with a forced grin, and walked away before she gave in to temptation and snuggled up beside him on the sunbed.

During the course of the weekend Rob seemed to relax, and with relaxation came trust and respect for Jamie. In turn, that helped her to find her feet and by the Monday morning she felt so at home she could have been born there.

Mrs Harrison was back, and Jackie came in and sighed in despair at the state of her old office.

'What a mess, Dr Buchanan!' she chided and he had the grace to blush.

'Sorry, Jackie. Just sort of ran away with me——'

'What about all the forms?'

He looked perplexed.

'Forget it!' she said with a laugh. 'Just go away and leave me alone with it for a wee while. I'll soon have it straight.'

So they left her to it, and by lunchtime the room was transformed. She explained the system to Jamie, and between them they worked out a suitable timetable for Jackie's hours, to fit in with them on the three days they were both at the surgery. On Tuesday and Friday one of them would be at Glenlivie, and it was decided that this could be a good time for the doctor left behind to catch up on form-filling and so on to fuel Jackie's hours. By the time Rob came in at lunchtime all that was required was his rubber stamp, in effect.

'I'm impressed,' he said, looking doubtful. 'Will I get into trouble if I lose anything?'

'Murderous trouble!' Jackie said threateningly, and Jamie tried not to laugh.

'Don't look so dismayed, Rob,' she soothed. 'If you give it two or three hours a week you should easily keep on top of it.'

'Damn silly contract,' he mumbled, and stomped off.

The two young women exchanged a smile at his expense.

In fact it did work well, and by the end of Jamie's second week the surgery was looking much more organised and businesslike.

Not all was plain sailing, however. Rob was worried about Mrs Douglas, who was not progressing well. They had cleared up her urinary tract infection, but she was now troubled by spasticity in one arm, and general fatigue. All in all, the prognosis was not good, although it was possible that she might have an unpredictable improvement and regain some or all of her lost functions. However Rob wasn't hopeful, and his concern for Trudy deepened with every day that passed.

She had been transferred to the dialysis unit in Inverness, and, although she was due to come home at the end of the week, with her mother in hospital they had agreed to keep her in, but she was miserable and homesick. Both Rob and Jamie had been to visit her, taking turns, and one or two schoolfriends had made the long trip to Inverness at the weekend, but she was still very alone and unhappy

They were in the little sitting-room on Friday evening

after supper, Jamie reading, Rob staring morosely out of the window, when Jamie decided he ought to be encouraged to talk about it.

'Difficult one, isn't it?' she said quietly.

'Hmm?' He swivelled round towards her, his eyes troubled.

'Trudy.'

He shook his head and sighed deeply. 'Jamie, I don't know what to do. I wish I could have her here. She's so unhappy in the hospital, so far from her mother—at least if she was here with me I could take her to visit her mum.'

'You miss her, don't you?'

He nodded. 'Yes,' he agreed heavily. 'I miss her. I love her very dearly. She's just like another daughter.'

'I thought so. Any idea when they'll be sending her mum home?'

'None. Not for a while. I wonder if we could have Trudy home here for the weekend?' He unwound himself from the chair and went to the phone in his study. Jamie listened to the conversation, and was unsurprised when he came back in and asked her if she could handle surgery in the morning.

'I'll leave at six and go and get her. I can't stand back and do nothing.'

'Just a pussycat,' Jamie said quietly, and he gave a hollow laugh.

'Who, me?'

'Yes, you,' she said with a smile.

Suddenly the tension was back in the air between them, and the awareness that they had both struggled to ignore refused to go away.

At last Rob dragged his eyes away from hers and went out into the garden.

'Think I'll do some digging,' he flung over his shoulder, and she left him to it. Perhaps a bit of physical activity would quieten him down. She half considered going out to join him, but decided that would be counter-productive. She settled instead for watching him through the window while he attacked the unsuspecting ground, which did wonders for her heart-rate but precious little for her peace of mind!

He picked Trudy up in the morning and took her to visit her mother. By the time they arrived back Jamie had finished surgery and done several visits, and she came in shortly after them. There was a delectable aroma of home cooking in the air, and she found Rob, Chloe and Trudy settled in the kitchen in front of a pile of home-made griddle scones and a mountain of fresh butter. Mrs Harrison was glowing gently at the stove, and Jamie grinned at her.

'Feeding of the five thousand?'

The housekeeper gave a short laugh. 'Something like that. Trudy's choice of lunch menu. There's a nice salad for you in the fridge, hen.'

'Thanks.' She found the salad and eyed the steadily growing mound of scones at the table. 'Need a hand?' she asked, and laughed as Mrs H rolled her eyes.

'You eat your lunch, Dr Cameron, while the phone's quiet. I can manage this lot.'

Jamie tousled Trudy's hair, and pulled up another chair to the table. 'How are you doing, young lady?'

The little girl shrugged and grinned. 'OK. It's great to be back here. The food in the hospital is yuck!'

Jamie laughed. 'I'm sure it's not, but it must be very difficult catering for all those hundreds of people every day. I expect it's OK when it leaves the kitchens.'

Rob's lips closed around another griddle scone, and he sighed with satisfaction. 'Can't be this good,' he said happily, and Chloe squirmed on his lap and reached for another.

'More!' she said, and stuffed it into his mouth.

He ate it obligingly and neatly fielded any further attempts to feed him by giving her one of her own to eat. Jamie watched in fascination as Trudy leaned over and brushed a crumb from Chloe's cheek.

Rob smiled at Trudy and gave her a hug, and she snuggled into his side with a sigh of contentment.

Jamie felt ludicrously left out, and made a great production of clearing the table and helping Mrs Harrison sort out the mess.

It was a wonderful afternoon, mild and sunny, and Rob took both girls down to the rocky shore to play in the rock-pools. She went to join them at one point and had to endure having her finger 'kissed' by a sea anemone, admire a jellyfish like a transparent saucer and count all the barnacles on a rock.

They were at three hundred and eighty seven when Mrs Harrison called Rob from the door.

'Call for you, Dr Buchanan.'

'I'll take it—I can't count above four hundred,' Jamie said with a grin and left him to it. Despite the warmth of the day and the delightful company of the children, she was almost relieved to go, because her imagination had strayed into fantasy, and she had allowed herself to believe, for a while at least, that they were just like any other family spending a day at the beach.

Rob did the calls that night, and she woke at one point to hear soft voices from the room next door. Getting up quietly, she tiptoed to the bathroom and on the way back she heard Trudy say, 'But she will die one day, won't she?'

'Everybody has to die some time, sweetheart,' Rob said gently, his voice a reassuring rumble in the lonely night. 'I expect your mum's got a good few years ahead of her yet.'

'Will I have to go into a children's home? Nobody will want to adopt me, will they? They want healthy children—I saw a programme on the telly and they said sick and disabled children were the hardest to find homes for—do you think they'll find a home for me, Dr Rob?'

Jamie heard the bed creak, and then Rob's voice muffled now, and even deeper than usual, replied, 'There'll always be a home for you here, darling, no matter what. Whenever you need me, I'll be here for you. Anyway, as I said, hopefully it'll be years before we have to worry.'

Jamie, moved almost to tears by the heartbreaking exchange, slipped quietly down the stairs and let herself into the kitchen. She put the kettle on and waited, and sure enough, a few minutes later Rob came down, still dressed from the last visit, his face taut with emotion.

'I heard,' she said gently, and opened her arms. He stepped towards her and wrapped her in a wordless hug, drawing comfort from her understanding, and then he released her and sat heavily down at the table, laid his head on his arms and sighed.

'She shouldn't have to deal with all that,' he said raggedly. 'No child should have to come to terms with the lingering death of a parent and the unknown horror of what happens next. The awful thing is she's right—nobody will want her, she's too much trouble.'

'You want her.'

'Aye.' He lifted his head and she saw the tears on his lashes. 'Aye, I want her, but will they let me have her, if it comes to that? I've promised her, Jamie. What if the authorities say no? I just hope to God it never happens.'

'That's unrealistic,' she said quietly.

He nodded. 'Sometimes we need to be, just to survive.'

They drank their tea in silence, both deep in thought, and before they had finished the phone rang again.

'Hi-ho, hi-ho,' Rob muttered wearily, and went into the surgery. Two minutes later he stuck his head round the door. 'Thanks for the tea and sympathy, love. I'll see you for breakfast.'

He gave her a tired smile that didn't manage to dispel the haunting sadness in his eyes, and then she heard the front door close behind him and the Land Rover roared into life.

Between them they got through the next day, and in the late afternoon Rob left for Inverness again with Trudy beside him. He took Jamie's car so she would have the Land Rover for the visits. So many of the patients lived off the beaten track that it was only sensible to use a rugged vehicle, but Jamie hated driving it and ground the gears repeatedly.

She was on her way back from a visit to one of the outlying farms when it started to rain, and the night seemed suddenly as black as ink. She rounded a corner and there on the road in front of her were two green eyes in a shapeless bundle. She had no chance of stopping, or even swerving, but as she went over it there was no thump or jolt. She slammed on the brakes and the Land Rover screeched and slithered to a halt at the side of the road.

Grabbing the torch, she leapt out into the lashing rain and ran back along the road to where she had seen the animal. It was a little dog, still lying where it had been, sodden and bedraggled, but remarkably she seemed to have missed it. However, it was possible that someone else had hit it, or soon would, so her first priority had to be to get it off the middle of the road and into the Land Rover, and take it to a vet.

Taking off her coat, she lay it on the ground and rolled the dog carefully on to it, and then dragged it to the side of the road. Leaving the torch there to mark the position, she ran back to the Land Rover and reversed it back to the dog, and then with some difficulty she lifted the dog into the back. It whimpered once, and she reached out to stroke it, but it cowered, as if expecting to be hit, and so she dropped her hand and spoke softly, reassuringly, before securing the back and climbing in behind the wheel.

She decided to go back to the surgery and call a vet from there, and by the time she arrived she was relieved to see her car back on the drive.

She went in and called Rob, and was outside again and opening the back door of the Land Rover by the time he emerged.

'What's up?' he asked.

'Can you help? I found a dog lying in the road—we need to call a vet——'

He was at her side, easing the dog gently into his arms and carrying it to the house before she had finished speaking.

She followed him into the kitchen and watched anxiously while he ran gentle hands over the dog's back and legs.

'Nothing obviously broken, but the poor wee thing's frozen—you too, Jamie. Go and get something dry on; I'll deal with this.'

She ran upstairs, washed her muddy hands quickly and threw on some dry clothes. Not stopping to dry her hair, she ran back down to the kitchen and knelt beside the shivering animal.

'Poor thing, he's miserable, but he didn't seem thin, really,' she said.

'She,' Rob replied drily, 'and the reason she didn't seem thin is because she's extremely pregnant. I can't find anything obviously wrong with her, but I've called the vet and he'll be here soon. Where did you find her?'

Jamie described the place, and Rob frowned. 'There's no one lives near there that I know of. I wonder whose she is? She's some kind of collie cross, I think—perhaps she's a sheepdog, but they're usually well cared for.'

Jamie reached out her hand and stroked the dog's

head gently. 'Poor girl,' she crooned softly, and the dog raised her head a little and licked her hand feebly. 'Oh, Rob, do you suppose she'll be all right?'

He shrugged. 'I don't know, love. Have you got a hairdrier we could use to dry her off a bit?'

She went and found it, and they had just finished when the vet arrived.

He examined her deftly, said he could find nothing wrong bar long-standing neglect and ill-treatment and the fact that she was near to term, gave her a vitamin injection and left.

Rob was on call so they stayed up together until half-past ten, and then he went off to bed to catch as much sleep as possible, and Jamie sat with the dog in the kitchen, watching as she slept restlessly by the stove. At a quarter to twelve she staggered to her feet and whined, and Jamie took her out into the garden and watched as she relieved herself. When she came back in she lay down again, exhausted by the effort, but not for long, rising again to pace restlessly.

'What's wong, old girl?' Jamie said gently, and the dog laid her head on Jamie's knee and whined softly. 'Oh, darling. Are you in a strange place? Is that the matter?'

The dog wagged her tail feebly and Jamie stroked her soft ears. 'Poor girl. What shall we call you, eh? Bess?'

The little collie wiggled her tail again, and Jamie smiled. 'Like that, do you? Shall we call you Bess?'

The dog left her side and went to the door again, and Jamie let her out, but she wasn't long, merely sniffing around the doorway and hauling herself awkwardly back inside after a few moments.

This time she returned to her place on Jamie's coat, and washed herself meticulously, particularly in the genital area and down the long rows of swollen teats.

'Oh, Bess, you can't do this to me!' Jamie murmured softly, and watched closely as the dog paused, as if waiting, before continuing to wash.

Twenty minutes later there was no doubt in her mind. Bess was in labour, and Jamie was condemned to a sleepless night.

The phone rang, and a few minutes later Rob stuck his head round the door. 'Call,' he said succinctly. 'How is she?'

'In labour,' Jamie said drily, and he rolled his eyes.

'Don't we have enough problems?' he muttered, and then grinned. 'How's your obstetric experience?'

'About to be enlarged!' she replied with a smile. 'Go on, be quick and come and give me a hand.'

He wasn't very long, only about half an hour, and there was no change, but he sat with Jamie anyway, drinking tea and talking quietly.

At one Bess started shifting restlessly again and pacing, and tried to go behind the fridge.

'I think she's probably looking for somewhere dark to go,' Jamie said thoughtfully, and Rob stood up and went out, returning moments later with an old cardboard box and a table lamp. He rigged up the lamp, turned off the top light and lay the box on its side with Jamie's coat inside it.

Immediately the dog crawled inside and turned

round and round a few times before settling down to her obsessional washing again.

They sat on the floor with their backs against the cupboards so they could keep an eye on her, and after a while their conversation dwindled and they sat in companionable silence.

It was chilly on the floor, and when Jamie shivered Rob shifted closer and tucked her into his side, his arm draped comfortably around her back and his hand resting on her hip.

'Go to sleep if you like,' he murmured, his voice very close to her ear, and she yawned at the thought and snuggled into his warmth.

'You're very comfy to lean on,' she said sleepily. 'I thought you'd be all unyielding and bony, but you're just right.'

'I'm very glad to hear it,' he replied, a thread of laughter in his voice. 'If I may say so, you feel just right, too!'

She giggled and turned her face round towards him. 'Thank you. That's the nicest thing anybody's said to me for hours!'

He chuckled. 'You're an idiot, Dr Cameron,' he told her, and then something shifted in his face and her heart caught in her throat.

'I think you ought to be warned that I'm about to kiss you very soundly,' he whispered, and, sliding his other hand under her thighs, he lifted her easily on to his lap. Then he ran his hands lightly up her sides, lingering at the soft outer swell of her breasts, and watching her intently as she caught her bottom lip between her teeth.

'Rob. . .'

He kissed her then, his big hands sliding on up to cup her head and steady it. After a while his mouth left hers and trailed tiny, biting kisses over her jaw and down the valley of her throat.

He must have felt her pulse rocket, and heard the breath catch in her throat, because his lips returned to hers, claiming her with a devastating passion that made her senses reel.

'I want you,' he murmured against her lips, and she squirmed against him, straining to be closer, so close——

'I thought you said you didn't want this,' she said raggedly.

'Damn that,' he muttered, 'I lied. God, Jamie, you feel so good——'

His hand left her hair and hovered lightly over her breast, so lightly that she wasn't sure if it was just imagination. She shifted against him and he groaned, his fingers closing gently over the soft flesh. 'Dear God, sweetheart—take this off, I want to see you, touch you, taste you. . .'

He raised the hem of her sweatshirt and drew in his breath sharply as he realised she was wearing nothing underneath it. Then his lips were closing over her nipple and the moist warmth of his mouth made her want to cry out.

She didn't realise that she had until he lifted his head and brushed her lips with his.

'Tell me what I do to you,' he muttered raggedly. 'I want to hear it all, every gasp, every sigh—hell, what are we doing on the kitchen floor? Let's go to bed.'

He stood up easily with Jamie in his arms, but his words had penetrated the haze of passion and she stared at him in horror.

'Rob, no! The dog!'

He stared back at her for several seconds, as if he was trying to make sense of her words, and then with a groan he closed his eyes and lowered her to her feet, sliding her intimately down his front.

'Just so you know what you do to me,' he said unsteadily.

She wrapped her arms around his waist and held on tight, reluctant to let him go. She was well aware of what she was doing to him, but she thought it was probably just as well that he couldn't tell what he had done to her—because, she realised with devastating clarity, what he had done was make her fall in love with him. Headlong, irretrievably, totally beyond her control. And, she realised with a sick sense of dread, it would be the very last thing he would want.

CHAPTER SIX

As the dog whimpered in her box, they released each other, each reluctant for his or her own reasons, and turned their attention to their patient.

Rob, with a rueful grin, crouched down and peered into the box.

'I think we're in business,' he said quietly, and Jamie looked over his shoulder.

'I can't see,' she whispered, and he shifted slightly and pulled her closer, hard up against his side. Her emotions were tumbling in confusion, part of her desperate to be so close to him, another part, maybe the saner, wanting to run away.

Then Bess strained down and a small, grey-wrapped parcel appeared. The dog immediately and instinctively tore open the membrane and licked the tiny bundle, but without success.

'Stillborn, I think.'

'Oh, Rob, are you sure?'

He reached into the box and lifted out the lifeless puppy. 'I'm afraid so. You could wrap it up and rub it with a warm tea-towel, or swing it by the legs like the shepherds do the lambs, but I doubt if it will do any good.'

They tried everything, but to no avail. A short while later the next was born, also stillborn, but then to their delight and surprise an hour later the third puppy to be born wriggled immediately. Bess, her maternal instinct revived by success, licked it ferociously and it sneezed.

'Oh, Rob, it's alive!' Jamie cried, and he hugged her.

'Tiny, isn't it? Wonder if there'll be any more live ones or if that's it?'

They settled down to wait, watching Bess as she nudged the puppy up to her teats, where it immediately began to suck vigorously.

'Instinct is a wonderful thing,' Rob murmured, watching her with an indulgent smile on his face. Bess continued to clean up the puppy as it suckled, and then the placenta came away a short time later.

They continued to watch her, but she settled down, exhausted, only stirring to lick the puppy occasionally.

'That's it, then,' Rob said, straightening his stiff limbs. 'One live puppy. Thank God for that. Sometimes they have ten or eleven!'

Jamie eyed Bess sceptically. 'I'm not sure she could support more than one.'

'I'm not sure I could stand more than one. I suppose we ought to find out who owns her.'

Jamie looked aghast. Scrambling to her feet, she caught his arm in entreaty. 'Rob, you can't send her back!'

'I can't keep her, Jamie. I've got more than enough to worry about already. She'll have to go——'

'I'll look after her! You can't be so cruel as to send her back——'

'Jamie, we can't keep her without trying to find the owner——'

'But he'll probably drown the puppy and he'll beat her and starve her and she'll probably die——'

'All right, all right! I'll see if I can find the owner and talk to him. OK?'

Jamie released his arm and reached up to kiss his cheek. 'Thank you, Rob,' she said huskily. 'I promise I'll take care of them both.'

'Humph. Till you leave——'

'I'm not going anywhere!'

'Not this again! Jamie, I'm too tired. I'm going to bed, and I suggest you do the same. Knowing our luck tomorrow will be a hell of a day.'

He left her then, and, after tidying up the box and leaving fresh water for Bess, Jamie followed him up the stairs.

Sleep, however, was the last thing on her mind as she lay down. Determinedly she closed her eyes, but all she could see was his face before he kissed her, and the imprint of his body on hers was so real that she could almost fool herself he was there. With a groan she rolled her face into the pillow and let her imagination run riot.

Mrs Harrison took the dog and her puppy in her stride, shifting the box out of the way and finding fresh blankets.

'I think your coat has probably had it, my dear,' she told a weary Jamie at breakfast.

'It doesn't matter, it was only an old anorak. How are they?'

'Och, fine—Mum seems quite well, and the puppy's

certainly latched on to the business of eating without any difficulty. Where did you find the poor wee thing?'

She was just describing the location when Rob walked in, looking as shattered as she felt but nevertheless devastatingly sexy in dark green cords and a green and navy plaid shirt. Quelling her clamouring senses, she forced herself to greet him calmly and then continued to tell Mrs H about the rescue.

'Nearest farm to that is old Roddy McIver—wicked to his dogs, he is. Usually keeps one tied up next to the road to keep the sheep from straying off the land—he ought to put in a cattle grid, but he's so tight he probably can't remember what his wallet looks like.'

'I'll go and see him, threaten him with the RSPCA and ask if we can keep the dog,' Rob said, giving Jamie a sideways look.

'He'll charge you, mind. Tell you what a valuable dog she is and how he'll do you for theft—you see if he doesn't!'

Mrs Harrison put their breakfast down on the table and bustled out to dress Chloe.

'Pay him if he wants money,' Jamie said, 'I'll pay you back, but don't let him have her, Rob.'

He sat next to her and her pulse rocketed out of control. 'Say please,' he teased gently, laughter sparkling in his eyes.

'Pretty please with a cherry on top?' she said with a winning smile, and his face cracked as he laughed, a great, hearty laugh that made her heart turn over.

'I'll do what I can, Jamie, I promise. Now eat your breakfast like a good girl——'

'I'm not a good girl——'

'I noticed,' he said, the smile in his eyes replaced by a hunger unabated by sleep. Suddenly he shot his chair back and stood up, walking over to stare out of the window. 'God, this is ridiculous. I haven't felt like this since I was about nineteen.'

Jamie had never felt like it in her life, but she wasn't about to tell him that. Martin's tepid attempts to interest her in a physical relationship had left her passive and unmoved, but Rob. . .! One look, one kiss, and she turned into a raving siren!

Fortunately she was saved by Mrs Harrison, who bustled back in, took one look at Rob's plate and told him in no uncertain terms to sit down and finish his breakfast.

'Yes, Mum,' he said dutifully.

'Don't you "yes, Mum" me, you great ox! Eat before you fall to bits. What good are you to your patients with neither food nor sleep? And who is doing the calls tonight?'

'It's my turn,' Jamie said wearily.

'Fine, so you need to go back to bed after surgery this morning and rest until the ante-natal clinic, and you——' she turned to Rob, her forefinger wagging '—you need to be in bed by ten at the latest. If you ask me, at the moment anyone trusting either of you with their health is taking their life in their hands. Now, Chloe love, how about some lovely Ready-Brek?'

Thus dismissed, they exchanged rueful grins and finished their breakfast in silence.

In fact it was a relatively easy day, and while Jamie was resting Rob went out and tackled Roddy McIver on the subject of Bess.

When Jamie came downstairs at two, she found Rob sitting on the kitchen floor tempting Bess with scraps of chicken and dog biscuit, while the puppy slept in a ball by her side.

'Hi,' he said softly.

She crouched beside them all. 'Did you find him?'

'Oh, aye. Mean old skinflint. Said she was his best sheepdog, and he wanted twenty quid or he'd report me to the police, so I told him that the vet had been very interested and that the RSPCA would probably press charges, so he changed tack and said she always was a damn nuisance, constantly running away, and I was welcome to her, puppy and all.'

Jamie was delighted. 'So we can keep her?'

'Looks like it.'

'Oh, Rob, that's wonderful! Oh, thank you!'

She flung her arms round him and hugged him, then lost her balance and ended up on his lap.

'I get a feeling of *déjà vu*,' he said softly, and shut his eyes. Jamie wriggled off his lap and he groaned quietly. 'One day, young lady,' he murmured, but Mrs Harrison came in with Chloe and she was saved again.

Chloe was fascinated, but Rob wouldn't let her touch the puppy. She patted Bess's head, though, and giggled delightedly. The soft thump of Bess's tail told them that she, too, thought it was rather nice getting all this attention, and Rob smiled in resignation.

'Always said you should get a pet for her,' Mrs Harrison said with satisfaction, and Rob groaned.

'I get the feeling I'm heavily outnumbered here,' he said with irony, and, levering himself to his feet, he swung Chloe up into his arms and took her out into the garden.

Jamie got slowly to her feet and exchanged a smile with the housekeeper.

'Any chance of a late lunch?'

The week passed quietly enough. On the medical front Mrs McKay seemed to be recovering slowly from her fall, Mrs Douglas came home from hospital and Trudy joined her, and the result of Josie Reeve's scan showed no abnormalities or pelvic disproportion. The dates seemed about right for the head size, and the only problem was the posterior presention, which, as Rob had said, might correct itself.

On a personal level Jamie tried to avoid being alone with Rob, spending more time in her room in the evenings when Chloe was in bed and Mrs Harrison had gone up to watch her television, and keeping their daytime exchanges to professional matters.

It didn't stop her loving him, though, and the more she saw of him with patients, the more her admiration and love grew.

And then there was Chloe.

Jamie adored the child, and found herself spending more and more time with her when Rob was out on calls or over at the branch surgery. Bess had attached herself firmly to Jamie, and so whenever she went into the kitchen the dog would get to her feet and come over to see her, wagging her tail and gazing adoringly up at Jamie. She lapped up affection, and Jamie guessed that she had been starved of it in the past.

Chloe, of course, thought the dog was a wonderful

toy, and yet she was consistently gentle with Bess, never pulling her tail or ears as small children often did. As the days passed the puppy grew more interesting, losing that bald look and opening its eyes, and by the beginning of the following week its eyes were opening and it was beginning to totter about.

By the end of the second week the puppy was getting playful, and Chloe was totally fascinated.

One evening Rob came back from a call to find Jamie sitting on the kitchen floor with Bess leaning against her leg, both watching as Chloe and the puppy played together on the rug in front of the stove.

Chloe offered the puppy a bit of biscuit and Jamie took it away, giving it instead to Bess.

'She's a baby, darling, she can't eat biscuits yet,' Jamie explained, but Rob picked the child up and carried her to the sink.

'No!' Chloe screamed. 'Puppy!'

'No, you have to wash your hands and go to bed now,' Rob insisted.

He washed the protesting child's hands and carried her out with a disapproving look on his face, and Jamie sighed. Now what? Was she to be accused of stealing the child's affections, putting her in danger from the dog's germs or some other imagined insult that his twisted mind had conjured up?

Too fraught to care, she returned the puppy to the box, let Bess out into the garden and washed her own hands. A few minutes later Rob came down to find her in the sitting room watching the news.

'I don't think it's a good idea for her to play with the puppy,' he said immediately.

'I'm sorry, I didn't think it would do her any harm, and I would have washed her hands——'

'Nevertheless, I don't want it happening again,' he told her curtly.

'Don't want what happening, exactly? Playing with the puppy, or playing with me? What is it that you don't want for her, Rob? Isn't she to be allowed to enjoy her childhood? Just because you don't have time to be with her always, does that mean the child has to be bored and understimulated when you aren't around? Just how big is your ego anyway?'

Her voice had risen until she was almost shouting, and his face tightened with anger.

'Who the hell are you to judge? And if you're so damn maternal, where are your children? Where's the loving husband and the two point four kids and the Labrador and the cottage in the country, Jamie?' he jeered.

Staggered by the unprovoked attack, she stood up awkwardly and made her way to the door, her usual grace deserting her. 'I'm sorry,' she said stiffly. 'She's your daughter; of course you have a right to say how she should be brought up and what she should and shouldn't do. I'm sorry I interfered. Goodnight.'

'Jamie, wait!'

She ignored him and walked blindly towards the stairs.

'Jamie, come back.'

'For more insults? No thank you, Rob. I'll see you in the morning.'

She left him in the hall, staring up at her, and as she reached the landing she heard him mutter, 'Damn you, then. Bloody women.' Moments later the sitting-room door slammed.

She crawled into bed, totally defeated, and lay staring at the ceiling. Four weeks of her two-month trial period were over, and she had only a few more weeks to go. Perhaps she'd make it.

And perhaps not. It was another sleepless night.

The following day there were gale warnings on the weather forecast, and when Rob came back from the branch surgery he reported that the road conditions had deteriorated.

'There's a lot of debris, little trees down and so on, and it really is very risky out there. I hope to God we don't get many calls.'

It was a vain hope. They covered the calls as they came in, both of them working so that they could be dealt with as quickly as possible before conditions got any worse. By the evening only a lunatic would have ventured out, and the news was full of stories of cars being blown off roads, caravan sites devastated and chimneys down. Rob rang the police and was told that the road to Fort William was closed, and that no ferries were running.

'Hope no one needs hospitalisation,' he said heavily.

Jamie, still hurting from his treatment the night before, said little, but like him she was concerned for the welfare of any patients needing urgent hospital treatment.

'I'll do the night,' he said firmly, and Jamie was only too glad to agree. She had no desire to venture out into the raging wind, gusting as it was to force twelve.

A trawler had been sunk, lost with all hands on the mountainous seas, and she stood by the office window and watched the waves lashing against the rocks. The shrubs in the garden were thrashing themselves to shreds against the walls, and the flowers were flattened, their petals smashed by the pelting rain.

As she stood there in the gathering gloom, the phone rang and Rob, coming into the office behind her, picked up the receiver.

'Hello, Sandy,' he said, and Jamie turned to watch him. As a frown creased his brow, her heart sank. Surely Josie Reeve wasn't going to choose tonight to go into labour?

But she was. While she listened to his instructions, she jotted down a list of things he would need to take, and as he came off the phone, she handed it to him.

'Can you think of anything else you'll need?'

He raised his eyes from the list, and the ghost of a smile touched his mouth.

'The luck of the devil. If I even get to her it'll be a miracle. Why tonight? Why not last night, or tomorrow?'

Jamie, her heart pounding with fear for him, went into the dispensary and started to assemble the necessary drugs: oxygen, Entonox and so on. Sterile maternity packs, forceps, sutures—the list seemed endless.

He came in behind her and checked the supplies. 'I can't get hold of the midwife—I think she's out with another patient and her husband says he expects her to stay there until the wind dies down.'

Jamie eyed him worriedly. 'Will you need help?'

He shrugged. 'Hopefully not. Who knows? With any

luck the wind will drop and I'll get her into hospital in time—it's the first baby, and might take ages anyway.'

'Ring me when you get there,' she told him. He hesitated, then nodded.

'Phone lines might be down by then. Don't go out to anyone unless it's literally a matter of life or death. Understand?'

She nodded. Mrs Harrison was standing beside her with a handful of candles.

'Just in case,' she said, and handed them to him.

They watched as he opened the front door and was slammed back against the wall by the force of the wind.

Then the door was shut, and he was gone.

'I hope to God he's all right,' she said fervently.

Mrs Harrison gave her a long, level look. 'Go with him,' she said. 'He may need you.'

She hesitated only a second, and grabbed her coat. He was just about to reverse off the drive when she wrestled open the door and climbed into the cab. 'I'm coming with you,' she yelled. 'You might need help and I don't fancy trying to get to you on my own.'

He met her eyes in the gloom. 'Sure? It'll be rough as hell, and pretty dangerous.'

'But you told me before you never get into trouble,' she yelled back with a grin.

His mouth twitched, and he laughed. 'Hang on tight, then,' he shouted, and then they were off.

It was only eight miles to the farm, but it seemed to take forever. Once they were off the coast road things improved a little, but still the Land Rover was buffeted about and twice Rob nearly lost control as the wind seemed to lift it and fling it around.

The lights in all the villages were out, and Jamie was only too glad that Mrs Harrison had thought to give them candles. Delivering a baby in the dark with forceps, which they would almost certainly have to do unless it had turned, would be virtually impossible.

'How much obstetrics have you done?' he asked as they approached the farm.

'Apart from the dog? Six months in a nice, sterile hospital environment with an SR and consultant to hand if things got tricky, and a ward sister who probably knew more about it than all the medical staff put together! How about you?'

He gave a short laugh. 'About the same. Ah, well, perhaps she'll surprise us and have a nice easy labour.'

He pulled up outside the little house and they gathered up all the equipment and battled through the wind to the front door.

'Thank God you're here!' Sandy said, his face a pale mask of worry. 'She seems to be making very heavy weather of it, and—I don't know, Doc, things don't seem quite right. You can tell—I know I've only delivered sheep, but—I think she's got problems.'

Rob laid a reassuring hand on his shoulder. 'Don't worry, Sandy. Let's get scrubbed up and have a look at her, eh? Dr Cameron, while I do that perhaps you'll go and have a chat and see if you can find out how she's coping?'

'Of course,' Jamie agreed, and headed for the little room at the back.

'Josie? Hello—remember me? Dr Cameron. How are you doing?'

The woman turned her pale, sweat-soaked face towards Jamie and tried to summon up a smile.

'Things seemed to be going OK, and then everything just ground to a halt.'

'How long have you been in labour?'

'About four hours, I think, but I've had twinges on and off over the last day or two, so maybe longer. Sandy was going to try to take me to hospital, but the police said the road was closed with the wind—trees down or some such—and so I had to stay, but I'm scared——'

She broke off and pressed her knuckles to her lips, fighting back the tears, and Jamie pulled off her coat and reached out a soothing hand to stroke her brow. 'You'll be all right now. We'll give you something for the pain and have a look to see what's holding things up. At least you've still got electricity.'

'It's a generator,' Josie told her. 'We're too isolated for mains. Times like this it has its advantages.'

Her face stiffened then and she cried out with pain. Immediately Jamie could see that she was fighting the contraction, and quickly rolled her on to her side.

'Just relax and try and breath gently up at the top of your chest—lovely, just like that. Little soft breaths—beautiful. That's better. Well done.'

Rob appeared then, his shirt-sleeves rolled up and a relaxing smile on his face.

'Another contraction?' he asked, and Jamie nodded. 'Good and strong, but she says nothing much is happening now.'

'Let's have a look, then,' he said to Josie, and she rolled on to her back and hitched up her nightie. His hands quickly outlined the position of the baby, and he nodded.

'Still a posterior lie, but that shouldn't be too great a problem. It's still a little bit early, so it won't be so big as it might have been, which will help. What about the heartbeat?'

He listened with the foetal stethoscope, and nodded. 'A hundred and ten. OK. Let's just have a look down here and see how your cervix is getting on, shall we?'

He opened a pack of sterile gloves and pulled them on, and then gave her a gentle but thorough internal while Sandy twitched around helplessly in the background.

Rob straightened and met Jamie's eyes. 'Coming on nicely,' he said, 'but I think we may have to try and encourage the babe to turn over. I'll need your help for that—come and scrub up with me and I'll sort out an injection for Josie.'

He smiled at the mother, winked at Sandy and ushered Jamie into the kitchen.

'Ever dealt with a deep transverse arrest?' he asked softly.

'Oh, no!' she whispered. 'Really?'

He nodded. 'I think the baby's tried to turn too late, and then jammed across the pelvis. You'll have to turn it manually.'

'What?'

He held up her hands, and then his. 'Look, Jamie. If I try and do it I'll wreck her pelvic floor, and my fingers probably won't fit round the sides of the head. We haven't got any Keillands forceps, there's no way she can go to hospital, and that hearbeat is far too low.

There's no sign of meconium yet, but it's only going to be a matter of time, and this wind isn't showing any signs of letting up. It's the only way. You scrub, I'll give her a pudendal block and an episiotomy, and we'll see what we can do.'

'But what if I'm not strong enough?' she wailed.

'You don't need strength, Jamie, you need the right action in the right orientation. Don't worry, love, I'll talk you through it. Just scrub.'

He left her to it, and by the time he returned she was gowned and scrubbed.

'Ready?'

'As I'll ever be.'

'Attagirl. Right, let's go over it. First of all I want you to try and identify the presenting parts. I think there's a bit of oedema, so it's a little tricky, but you should be able to feel the posterior fontanelle on the mother's left side, and the anterior on her right. What I want you to do is to put your fingers under the baby's head, and your thumb on top, and turn the head so that your thumb comes over and down on your left—OK? Very gently, but you should manage. I've told them what we're going to do and why, and once the anaesthetic's working I'll do the episiotomy. OK?'

Jamie nodded. Her mouth felt dry, her hands were shaking and she was supremely terrified, but she wasn't going to feel any better until the baby was safely delivered. 'Let's go,' she said briskly, and led him back into the bedroom.

Josie gave her a tremulous smile, and she returned it, hopefully with a little more confidence.

'How are you doing?' she asked.

'OK. Have you done this before?'

Jamie flashed her a casual grin. 'I've delivered lots of awkward babies, Josie. I'm sure yours will be just as lovely as all the others.'

'I hope so,' the girl said worriedly.

'Are you numb now?' Rob asked, and she nodded.

'Right, I'm just going to do the episiotomy, so we've got plenty of space for all the manoeuvering, then Dr Cameron can have a go at turning this little beastie for you. Just relax, lass. I won't hurt you—there. All yours, Jamie. I'll try and turn the shoulder with you so it doesn't turn back.'

She took a deep breath to steady herself, and then carefully eased her hand in until she could feel the baby's head. Sure enough, it was wedged sideways across the pelvic outlet, and wasn't going anywhere without persuasion. Just then Josie had a contraction and the head pushed down hard against the sides of the pelvis. Josie moaned with pain and Sandy gripped her hand encouragingly.

She was conscious of Rob's body comfortingly close to her side, and as the contraction wore off he met her eyes and nodded.

'Ready when you are,' he said quietly, and gripping the baby's head gently, she tried to coax it round. At first it resisted, but then suddenly she felt the head shift.

'It's going,' she murmured, and he grinned.

'I know. I can feel it. Don't worry, I've got the shoulder. Now, once it's rotated can you get those forceps on, or do you want me to do it?'

'Can you? I'll hold the head and the shoulder, and you get the forceps in before I let go.'

She slid her hand under his on Josie's abdomen and wrapped her fingers round the point of the baby's shoulder.

'Just in case it tries to sneak back,' she said with a grin.

'OK,' Rob said, 'you can let go now, I've got the forceps on. One more good contraction and we should be in business.'

Moments later the baby's head came into view, and with a little lift and the smallest amount of traction, the head was delivered, followed almost instantly by the body.

They all held their breath for a second, and then the baby, obviously enraged at the insults that had been heaped upon his head, let out a lusty yell.

Josie burst into tears, Sandy went pink and hugged her hard, and Rob grinned.

'We did it,' he said quietly, and Jamie didn't know whether to laugh or cry.

'We did, didn't we?' she replied, and, lifting the squalling baby up, she laid him at Josie's breast.

'Congratulations,' she said huskily, and then she was crying too and didn't give a single damn, because the baby had so nearly died and she had been totally terrified and everything was now all right.

Rob's arms went round her in a wordless hug, and then they were dealing with the mundane chores of delivering the placenta and cleaning up the bed prior to suturing.

'Do you want to do this, or shall I?' Rob asked her.

'Oh, you do it,' she said with a laugh. 'I want to check over the baby and tidy up the mum and have a cup of tea!'

'Idle,' he said fondly, settling himself on the bed and beginning the tedious business of suturing. 'While you're making tea, think of the worker here.'

'I'll watch you,' she teased, 'and any granny knots and you don't get a cup.'

Finally they were finished, and by the time they were ready to leave the wind had dropped and the sky was clear. Josie was to stay at home with Sandy, and they promised to visit the following day to make sure everything was all right.

They travelled in silence for some time, and then when they reached the coast road Rob pulled over into a lay-by and switched off the engine.

'Come on, let's go for a walk,' he suggested, and she gladly agreed.

They walked side by side for a minute or two, and then Rob stopped and turned to face her.

'You did really well back there, Jamie,' he said quietly. 'If it hadn't been for you it might have been quite a different outcome. Thank God you came with me.'

'Oh, Rob, you're too kind. I was scared to death that it wouldn't work, and I could hardly get my fingers in between the head and her pelvis—I really didn't think it was going to work, you know.'

'Nevertheless, it did, thanks to you. And while I'm building up your ego at the expense of mine, I wanted to apologise for last night. I'm inclined to have tunnel vision where Chloe's concerned, and if I was unreasonable I'm sorry.'

She flashed him a little smile in the moonlight. 'That's OK, I'll forgive you.'

They walked back to the Land Rover then, and as they made their way back to the house Jamie thought how much things could change in such a short time. Less than twenty-four hours before she had been thinking that she wouldn't get through the next month, and now it seemed as if it wouldn't be long enough. Frankly, she didn't know which was worse.

CHAPTER SEVEN

By comparison with Friday night, the rest of the weekend was a walk-over. Jamie was profoundly relieved, because she was on duty and Rob, finally convinced that she could do the job as well as him, had taken Chloe away for the weekend to visit his parents.

Mrs Harrison spent Saturday shopping in Fort William for her niece's wedding the following weekend, and for the first time Jamie was alone in the house.

Normally she wouldn't have minded but this weekend, somehow, she felt very much alone. Bess was a comfort, and in a quiet moment she took the little collie out for a short walk along the shore to give her a break from the demands of her puppy.

The days were shorter now, and markedly colder as September drew to an end and October came with the blazing colours of autumn on the hills behind the house.

She gazed up at them longingly as the dog sniffed around among the rocks, and she thought how wonderful it would be to stroll hand in hand over the heather with Rob—because that was the trouble, of course. She missed him desperately, him and his little bundle of mischief that she wasn't supposed to love.

If only he would trust her and allow himself to love, how different things could be, she thought sadly, but there was no guarantee, of course, that he would love her anyway.

Restless and despairing, she called Bess and took her back to the house, where they were greeted enthusiastically by the lonely puppy.

Then the phone rang, and she went out on another call, and while she was out she checked on the Reeves and their new baby.

The midwife had been and expressed her delight at the new arrival, and Sandy seemed to have grown even taller overnight. He answered the door to Jamie with his son asleep in his arms, and she had to stifle a smile at the sight of the big man with the tiny baby.

'You look very pleased with yourself,' she teased him gently, and he grinned, quite unabashed.

'He's a fine lad,' he said a little gruffly, and his callused forefinger came up and brushed the baby's cheek tenderly.

'How's Josie?' she asked.

'Oh, a bit sore—glad it's over, I think. So am I. I really thought for a while there we'd lost him. I'm glad you came—I wanted to thank you for what you did.'

She shrugged and smiled. 'It was nothing, Sandy. Dr Buchanan would have managed quite well without me, you know.'

'Aye, well, in a pinch I dare say I could have turned the babe myself, but I'm happier with sheep! The fact remains you did it, and I'm grateful.'

Jamie was touched, and her face flooded with soft colour. 'You're welcome,' she said diffidently, and then gave in to impulse.

'Mind if I have a cuddle with the little lad?'

He laughed. 'Of course not. Have you got time for a cup of tea?'

'No, not really. I'd like to see Josie, and then I'll get out of your way.' He handed over his precious bundle and led the way through to the bedroom.

Jamie smiled down at the baby who was watching her with solemn eyes. 'Hello, precious. What's your name going to be?'

'Jamie, the same as you,' Josie told her. 'It's my grandfather's name, but under the circumstances it seems very appropriate!'

'Well, young James,' she said firmly, trying to disguise the wash of warmth that touched her at Josie's words, 'you look after your mum now, and let her get some sleep, eh?'

She handed him back to Sandy, checked Josie's blood pressure and TPR, and had a quick look at the stitches.

'Lovely bit of needlework,' she commented lightly as she straightened the bedclothes.

Josie laughed. 'I have no doubt I'll be grateful to him one day, but just now they're giving me a fair amount of discomfort.'

'That'll soon go. Little hint—sit on something hard rather than a soft cushion—it doesn't put so much stress on the sutures and tends not to hurt so much. I'm sorry we had to give you such an extensive cut.'

'He's safe—that's all that matters. I'll heal, Dr Cameron, given time. He didn't have time.'

Jamie nodded. 'All's well and all that. I must get back in case anyone else needs me. Call me if you're worried about anything. The midwife will be in every day at first, and we'll see you in six weeks if not before.'

Josie came to the door to see her off, and as she drove away Jamie turned back to wave.

They were standing in the doorway, Sandy's arm round Josie's shoulders, the baby in his other arm, and the hills behind were alight with gold and purple from the gorse and heather. It dawned on Jamie that she wouldn't be here when Josie came in for her post-natal check-up, and she felt a sudden and ridiculous lump in her throat.

She lifted her hand in a wave and then turned her eyes back to the road, blinking hard to clear her vision. Damn him for his stupid, stiff-necked attitude. She didn't want to move on, to go to some other practice and start all over again. This was home to her now, this wild and lovely country with its gentle, friendly people—all except the one man who really mattered, and all he wanted to do was to send her away.

She was kept reasonably busy for the rest of the weekend, and was curled up in a chair reading when the front door banged on Sunday evening.

She heard Chloe's excited chatter in the kitchen, and moments later the door opened and Rob came in.

He looked wonderful in soft old denims and an ancient flannel shirt rolled up over his tanned forearms, and her heart caught in her throat. She forced herself to react normally.

'Good weekend?' she asked conversationally.

'Lovely, thank you. How about you?'

'OK. Not too busy really. Josie and the baby are

doing well, and otherwise it was just minor bits and bobs—viruses, tummy upsets and so on. No admissions.'

'Good. Well, thanks for covering me. I feel much better for a break.'

'You look it,' she said, and as he met her eyes the tension was back.

End of polite conversation, she thought with dry humour, and dropped her eyes back to her book while her heart somersaulted in her chest. A few seconds later she heard the door open and close and then his voice sounded in the kitchen next door. He was there for quite some time, the deep rumble of his voice dragging her attention from her book, and then she heard his tread on the stairs as he put Chloe to bed.

Just when Jamie thought she might take herself upstairs to avoid him for the rest of the evening, he came back down and settled himself on the settee, arms draped over the side and back, long legs sprawled out and tugging the faded fabric of his jeans intimately over his thighs.

Jamie looked away and pulled her skirt down further over her knees.

'So, Dr Cameron, have you missed me?' he asked teasingly.

'Every minute,' she replied truthfully, and he laughed.

'Liar,' he murmured.

If you only knew, she thought with irony, and glanced up from her book. He was watching her intently, his eyes slightly hooded so that she couldn't read their expression, but she had the distinct feeling that he wanted it to be true. But why on earth would he want her to miss him when every waking minute he tried to convince her she would be leaving soon? Wishful thinking, she decided, and turned over the page blindly.

'Good book?'

She laid it down and sighed.

'I'm not getting the chance to find out,' she chided gently.

'Sorry,' he apologised, quite unabashed. 'Fancy a stroll round the garden?'

'OK.' She stood up and slipped her feet into her shoes. 'It'll clear my head before I go to bed.'

He opened the garden door and held it for her, and as she went through she caught the scent of soap and warm skin. It made her heart thump, and she was filled with a sudden yearning to lay her head against his chest and give in to her longing for him. Instead she moved away from him and walked across the grass, schooling her expression and subduing her racing pulse.

'Everything's thrashed to bits,' he said sadly, and, picking the tattered remains of a deep red rose, he lifted it to his face and breathed deeply. 'Such a shame,' he murmured, and before she could move, he tucked it behind her ear. Then he caught her hand in his and pulled her to his side as he strolled slowly round the garden inspecting the damage.

'There's nothing a good prune won't solve,' Jamie said comfortingly, 'and there's always next year.'

Except I won't be here to see it, and it was so pretty before the wind. She reached out and touched the broken stems of the chrysanthemums, and a deep sigh escaped her.

'Penny for them,' he murmured.

'Oh, I was just thinking about my mother. She used to grow chrysanths in the garden at home, and they were always being broken by the wind.'

'Where's home?' he asked, and, because she didn't feel like dealing with explanations, she told him it was in Sussex.

'On the Downs. Very exposed, especially at this time of year. After growing up there I hated living in towns.'

'You trained at Westminster, didn't you?'

'Yes—that wasn't too bad because there was always St James's Park or the Embankment, but I was very conscious of the press of people. Then I did my house year in Southampton, to be nearer home, and ended up in Birmingham for my GP trainee year. And now I'm here. . .'

No nearer to a permanent solution.

As if she had spoken out loud, Rob sighed and pulled her closer. 'I'm sorry, Jamie, but I really need a partner I can treat as an equal.'

'You could, if only you weren't so prejudiced!'

'I know I'm prejudiced, but I would worry all the time and end up doing all the night calls in winter and panicking every time you were out and it started snowing—you have no idea how inhospitable this country can be in the winter. People who don't know it can end up in difficulties so easily.'

'Not if they're sensible——'

'Anyway, given time you'd hate it. There's nothing to do, nowhere to go——'

'I haven't noticed—I've hardly had time to get bored!'

He regarded her seriously in the fading light. 'No, and that's my fault. Next weekend Mrs Harrison is going to her niece's wedding, and Chloe is going to stay with my parents. They're picking her up on Thursday evening and bringing her back on Monday. Why don't you go down to Sussex and stay with your parents? Take a long weekend—say Thursday to Monday. You could fly from Glasgow if you didn't feel like driving all the way.'

She shook her head helplessly. 'No, I—I can't.'

'Why? You don't have anything else arranged, do you? Are they away?'

Her throat was so choked she couldn't speak for a moment, so she shook her head.

'Jamie?' His voice was soft, his breath a sigh against her cheek. He lifted her chin and stared searchingly into her eyes. 'Tell me about it,' he said gently.

It was his gentleness that was her undoing. She closed her eyes and felt the tears slip down her cheeks, and then his arms were round her holding her against his chest, and his heart was thudding reassuringly under her ear.

She fought for a moment to hold back the tears, but the warmth of his body and the gentle movements of his hands against her spine broke through her resolve, and she let the tears fall silently against his shirt.

'Ah, love, what's wrong?' he murmured, soothing her with his big hands, and gradually she let the sobs come, great dry racking sobs dragged up from the depths of her misery and bringing with them all the buried pain.

And then finally the pain was gone, washed away by the cleansing tears, and Rob was blotting her face gently and regarding her with such tenderness that she nearly started all over again.

He led her to the stone seat tucked in under the climbing roses and pulled her down beside him, keeping his arm firmly round her shoulders. 'Talk to me,' he prompted, and so she did, telling him all about her mother's death from cancer at the age of thirty-eight, when she had been only thirteen, and how her father had thrown himself into his business and worked himself half to death.

'By the time he dared to lift his head and look around I was eighteen and at university, and he was all alone. His first wife had left him and taken his son, Mum had died and I had grown up and left the nest, and I don't think he knew how to cope. He threw himself back into business, and I spent as much time with him as I could, but then he started to be preoccupied and bad-tempered.

'Then suddenly this May he died, in the middle of a board meeting. It was totally unexpected, and it was only after he died that the true state of his finances came to light. You see, although the firm was a limited company, he'd mortgaged the house to inject more funds into the firm—it was badly affected by the recession, and only just survived.

'I had to sell the house and clear the contents, and then settle back and wait for what was left. I was appalled. He'd sold most of the valuable items, all the family silver, the clocks, the pictures—all of it, in the weeks before he'd died. Anything else of any value was sold, the mortgage was settled, the firm sold, and I ended up with a few thousand and a couple of cardboard boxes full of memories—that was when Martin high-tailed it out of my life,' she added so bitterly that Rob's eyebrows rose.

'Martin?'

She gave a brief, unladylike snort. 'My fiancé. He thought Daddy was rich as Croesus—the house in Sussex was worth close to half a million until lack of maintenance and the recession chopped a hole in its value, and by the time the firm was sorted out and shipped off to some vulture there was damn all left. He was unimpressed. As long as he'd thought he might be able to set himself up in private practice on the strength of the family money, he was content at least to make a pretence of being faithful. Once he knew the real situation—well, he didn't bother pretending any more. Told me no one in their right mind would want to marry me, I'd make a rotten wife, I was obsessed by my career—which was rich, coming from him!—and besides which, I was——'

She broke off, biting her lip.

'Besides which, you were what?'

'Frigid,' she said flatly.

Rob snorted. 'Meaning?'

She smiled wanly. 'Meaning I didn't react favourably to his intermittent overtures.'

Beside her, Rob gave a choking snort of laughter. 'We're a right pair, you and I,' he murmured sadly.

'My ex-wife told me in no uncertain terms that I was no good in the sack.'

Jamie stared at him in amazement. 'But that's ridiculous!'

'And how would you know?' he asked wryly.

She swallowed and dropped her eyes from his. 'Well, the way you kissed me——'

'Turned you on? Me too. And you responded to me, so you can't be frigid—God, I hate that word. How long did you sleep with him for? Six months? A year?'.

'I—I didn't—not completely.'

He looked at her in amazement. 'How long were you going out with him?'

She dropped her eyes. 'Four years.'

'Then the man was a fool. If you were going out with me for four years you'd damn well be in my bed. Damn it, I'm having enough trouble after four weeks!'

She met his eyes then, her own wide with shock and desire.

'I can't believe we're having this conversation,' she moaned softly.

'Neither can I—there are much better things we should be doing——'

'Rob, no!'

'Why?'

'Because—just because,' she finished lamely.

'Not good enough. We've beaten around the bush for too long as it is. Damn it, Jamie, we're both adults.'

She was trapped by his eyes, ensnared by the burning intensity of the desire that blazed in their midnight depths, and then just when she thought she would catch fire he pulled away with a sigh.

'Phone,' he muttered gruffly, and walked swiftly away from her.

She wasn't sure if she was relieved or not, but one thing was sure—it was just a temporary reprieve.

On Tuesday he went over to Glenlivie for the branch surgery and Jamie was able to concentrate properly for the first time since Sunday night. They had been busy, thankfully, and so avoiding him hadn't been the major tussle it might have been, but nevertheless it was a relief to be able to go into the kitchen after surgery and know he wouldn't be there.

Mrs Harrison gave her a keen look and plonked a cup of coffee down in front of her.

'Sit and drink it quick before the phone rings,' she ordered, and Jamie smiled and obeyed.

I wonder if she'd be so willing to tell me what to do about Rob, she thought idly, and stirred her coffee absentmindedly as her head conjured images of him to torture her.

Chloe was sitting on the floor patting Bess, and the puppy lay sprawled against her mother, snoring gently.

'Are they in your way?' Jamie asked, and Mrs Harrison shook her head.

'No problem, lass. The wee one is entranced—she doesn't want to do anything or go anywhere without the puppy!'

'Rob doesn't like her playing with it,' Jamie told her, and her eyebrows shot up.

'Really? While you were out last night he sat on the floor with Chloe and the puppy on his lap and encouraged her to stroke it. In fact, I don't know who was more taken with the wee thing; him or the bairn!'

'Oh.' Jamie felt deflated. Obviously, then, it was her and not the puppy he objected to—either that or he was paying attention to what she had said about denying Chloe experiences, and as that sort of minor miracle was unlikely, that left her as the stumbling-block.

'I must get on,' she said, and, draining her cup, she rose abruptly to her feet and left the room. Her eyes were stinging, and she dashed her hand over them just as Rob walked in through the front door.

'You're back early,' she said in surprise.

'Small turn-out. I dropped in on Mrs McKay. She doesn't look good.'

'Oh, no! She was doing so well—her cast is supposed to come off in a week—what's the matter with her?'

He shrugged. 'Weight loss, lack of appetite, loss of colour, no energy, low blood-pressure—nothing specific, but she's just sliding downhill.'

He looked desperately weary, almost defeated. Jamie reached out her hand and touched his arm.

'Is she dying?'

He met her eyes, his own searching hers as if he was looking for a way out, and then he looked away and nodded. 'I think so. She doesn't want to go back to hospital, and I think she's just given up. I've told her to ring if she needs one of us, and I'll get the district nurse to go in every day. I'll drop in whenever I'm over that way, but yes, I think this is it.'

He walked past her to his surgery, shutting the door

firmly behind him, and Jamie went back into the kitchen.

'Rob's back—would you take him in a cup of coffee in a minute? I'm going to do my calls now.'

It was a busy day, with plenty to keep them both occupied until after evening surgery. By the time she closed the front door after the last patient, Rob was upstairs having a shower and Chloe was tucked up in bed, singing to herself. Taking the coward's way out, she went into the kitchen, helped herself to her supper and took the tray up to her room.

As luck would have it, Rob emerged from his bedroom just as her foot hit the landing, and he rose one eyebrow in enquiry.

'Hiding?' he teased, but his heart wasn't really in it.

'No—I—my head aches. I thought I'd have a quiet evening as you're on call.'

'Good idea,' he said, and if she had expected him to protest she was going to be disappointed.

He stood back to let her pass and then ran lightly down the stairs to the kitchen.

Now what had she done? He looked so fed up—worried and saddened by Mrs McKay, no doubt, and she had put herself out of reach so that he had no opportunity to share the burden.

Her shoulders drooping with misery, and, torn between the desire to be with him and share his lows as well as his highs, and the urge to flee while she still had the chance, she didn't hear him come up behind her.

'What's up?' he said softly.

She turned slowly round. 'You need to talk, don't you?'

He met her eyes for an age, and then shook his head. 'Not talk, necessarily, but I could do with some company, and I thought maybe I could rub your neck and ease some of the tension.'

She almost laughed out loud. How he imagined that laying his hands on her neck would in any way relax her. . .

He took the tray from her and with a murmured, 'Come on,' led her downstairs and into the sitting-room.

There was a plate heaped with food on the coffee table, and he put the tray down next to it, sat her on the settee beside him and picked up his plate.

'Eat,' he mumbled, and so she did, pushing the food round on the plate with half-hearted prods of the fork until he took it out of her hands and pulled her down across his lap.

'Relax,' he told her gently, and then his warm, strong hands were kneading the tight muscles at the back of her neck. She let her head fall forwards, and felt the slight shift of his thighs beneath her cheek, the muscles relaxed, warm and firm against her face.

He was wearing the dark green cords again, the pile velvety soft, and she lifted her hand and rested it palm down beside her cheek. His leg tensed, and then he was lifting and turning her into his arms, his mouth finding hers hungrily in a searching kiss that wiped out all her resolve and left her trembling in his arms.

'God, Jamie, I don't know what you do to me,' he murmured, and then his mouth came down again, searching, demanding, his tongue insistent. She moaned low in her throat, and she felt his control snap as a shudder ran through him.

'Now, for God's sake, Jamie, please?' he breathed raggedly against her throat, and she nodded helplessly.

'Oh, yes,' she whispered. 'Oh, Rob, yes. . .'

He lifted his head and met her eyes, his own wild with need and yet full of a tender concern that convinced her as nothing else could that this was right.

'Not here,' he grated, and then in the silence the phone rang, shattering the tension.

He swore, quietly but comprehensively, and picked up the receiver.

'OK, I'll be right over,' he said after a moment, and Jamie wondered if anybody else could hear the huskiness in his voice. Then he turned to her, his eyes brimming with rueful laughter, and kissed her tenderly.

'Soon, Jamie—I promise.'

Then he was gone, leaving her emotions roiling round and her self-possession in tatters.

Reprieved again—but not for long. There was the weekend ahead, and she felt sure that the next time he wouldn't be distracted—even if he had to take the phone off the hook!

CHAPTER EIGHT

FOR the next two hectic days, the tension screamed between them, and every brush of Rob's hand against Jamie's, every glance, every murmured word stoked the fires that blazed out of control just under the surface.

On Thursday evening she was just coming out of the surgery when the phone rang. Rob answered it in the office, and went off on a house call mumbling something about Chloe and his parents.

Chloe and Mrs Harrison were in the kitchen feeding the puppy, and Jamie went to join them. Chloe immediately ran to her and dragged her over to join in.

'I'll pack her last few things if you could stay with her, Dr Cameron,' Mrs Harrison said, and so it was that Jamie was on the floor, her hair tucked behind her ears and Chloe and the puppy both squirming on her lap when there was a tap at the door and an elderly couple came into the room.

'G'ama!' Chloe trilled, and launched herself unsteadily across the kitchen floor.

Jamie struggled inelegantly to her feet, smoothed her hair back off her face and dumped the puppy back into the box with Bess.

As she straightened she looked up straight into a

pair of laughing eyes so familiar that they took her breath away.

'You must be Jamie,' the man rumbled in Rob's voice, and stuck out his hand. 'Angus Buchanan, and this is my wife Helen.'

Jamie shook his hand, and then turned to his wife. 'Hello. I'm sorry, Rob's not here at the moment—can I get you a cup of tea?'

Mrs Buchanan sank gratefully on to a chair at the table and hoisted Chloe on to her lap, heedless of the dog hairs and puppy smells on her immaculate fine wool skirt.

'Wonderful idea—I could murder a cup. Sorry we're late; we missed the ferry and had to wait half an hour at the Narrows—either that or drive another twenty miles on these awful roads!'

Jamie laughed. 'Yes, they are pretty dismal, aren't they? Still, the scenery makes up for it, and think, if they were any better people would be able to get here!'

His mother laughed. 'You sound just like Rob. He likes his isolation, too. Unlike——'

She bit her lip and turned away, but not before Jamie saw the pain in her eyes. So Jennifer's betrayal had hurt them, too. Not surprising, really, considering that she had abandoned their grandchild.

At that moment the child in question squirmed off her lap and headed for her grandfather, clambering up on to his lap and grabbing his hair to steady herself.

Then she turned round, plopped herself down on his lap and looked Jamie straight in the eye.

'Tea!' she demanded.

'Tea, please, Jamie,' she prompted, and Chloe giggled.

'Tea, p'ease, Jamie,' she piped. 'G'andad want tea? G'ama?'

'Everybody's having tea,' Jamie said firmly, and filled the kettle. 'How about a meal? Have you eaten?'

'No, lass, we'll have something later—how about the wee one? Has she had hers?'

Jamie glanced at Chloe's mucky little face and smiled at them. 'Judging by the look of her, she's had something that ended with chocolate pudding!'

'Choc'ate pudding—yummy!'

'I don't doubt it, darling,' Jamie said drily just as Rob walked in.

'Hi!' He bent and kissed his mother, laid a hand on his father's shoulder and tousled Chloe's hair.

'All ready, poppet? You're going to stay with Grandma and Grandad for the weekend—will that be fun?'

'Take puppy,' she said firmly.

'I don't think so, not this time,' Rob answered.

'Why?'

'Because she still needs her mummy, darling,' Jamie explained gently.

Chloe looked at her seriously for a moment, and then turned to her father.

'Chloe got a mummy?'

Jamie's heart wrenched at the anguish in Rob's eyes. He hunkered down beside his daughter, ruffled her hair and said softly, 'You have a mummy, darling. She just doesn't live here.'

Chloe eyed him thoughtfully. 'Why?'

He swallowed. 'Because she doesn't love me any more.'

Chloe swivelled round and her eyes settled on Jamie. Her little face lit up. 'Jamie be Mummy. Jamie love you.'

Their eyes met over the baby's head, his wild with despair, hers wide with shock. Her hand on her chest to steady the frantic beating of her heart, she backed away. Dear God, she thought, out of the mouths of babes——

'Of course she doesn't,' Rob said, and Jamie was shocked at the trace of bitterness in his voice. 'Anyway, Jamie's a busy doctor—she doesn't have time to be a mummy.'

Try me! she thought, and for a moment, as she met his mother's all-seeing eyes, she thought she must have said it out loud.

'I think the kettle's boiled, dear,' Helen said gently, and Jamie turned blindly away, grateful for the distraction.

Then Mrs Harrison came bustling down, and the phone rang, and Jamie took the call so that Rob could have tea with his parents and say goodbye to Chloe.

As she escaped gratefully from the house, Mrs Buchanan appeared at her side and laid a hand on her arm. 'Men are often blind,' she said gently. 'So often they can't see what's under their noses. Don't let it hurt you, Jamie. He'll come round. He's fighting it, but I think he's fallen for you in a big way. He's just too stubborn to admit it's true. Will you be here this weekend?'

Jamie met her eyes and flushed, but held her ground. 'Yes—yes, I will.'

'Take advantage of him,' his mother advised with a worldly twinkle. 'Don't let him win—he doesn't really want to.'

Then with a tiny wink she was gone, tall and elegant, the last person you would have expected to give that sort of advice.

Suddenly light-hearted, Jamie slid behind the wheel of her car and set off on her call.

By the time she came back Rob had gone out on a call, and he wasn't in again before she went to bed.

In the morning he dashed out just as she came down to breakfast, and she found a note on her desk.

> Take branch surgery, please—and visit Mrs McKay. Rob.

Shrugging, she loaded up the car with supplies from the dispensary and made her way to Glenlivie. The hall was full of patients, probably because Tuesday had been light and it was a nice day today. Nobody minded going out in the sunshine to visit the doctor! Oh, well, she thought, swings and roundabouts. At least it would keep her mind off Rob and the coming weekend!

It was lunchtime by the time she had finished with the last patient, and she grabbed a cup of tea before going off to do the home visits.

Mrs McKay was last on her list, and she arrived there at two, just as the sun came out and filled the glen with colour.

There was a pint of milk on the step and a black and

white cat appeared from nowhere and rubbed against her legs as she stepped from the car.

There was no answer to her knock, and she went round to the back door. It opened to her touch, and she went through to the sitting-room, calling as she went.

'Hello, lassie. Sorry I didn't come to the door. M'legs don't seem too good today,' Mrs McKay explained in a thin, shaky voice.

'That's all right, my love,' Jamie told her, smiling warmly. 'Let's have a look at you and see if I can get you a bit more comfy.'

She perched on the edge of the settee where the old lady was lying, her thin legs covered by a rug, and picked up her hand.

It felt like a bird, thin and frail, the skin so fine that she could almost see the bones. Her pulse was weak and thready, and she could hardly lift her head.

'When did you last eat?' she asked gently.

'Oh, Dr Buchanan gave me a cup of tea and a couple of biscuits last night when he popped in.'

'And what about today? Have you had anything today?'

She shook her head. 'Didn't fancy anything, hen. The nurse came and tried to make me eat, but—it's too late now to worry. Here, lass, hand me my work-basket, would you? I've got something for you.'

Puzzled, Jamie lifted the basket on to her lap and opened it. Inside, folded neatly, was a piece of patch-work, the stitches so tiny that they were all but invisible.

'I meant to put a back on it, but there wasnae time—

this cast slowed me down dreadful badly. Perhaps you can do that. Here, have it for your bottom drawer—if you put a wee bit o' blanket inside it'll keep you warm while he's away out on call all those chilly winter nights.'

'But, Mrs McKay, what about your family?'

She flapped her hand feebly in dismissal. 'They have nae use for my country ways—no, Dr Cameron, you have it, as a wedding present.'

She tried to smile. 'But I'm not getting married, Mrs McKay——'

'Och, lassie, of course you are. He just doesn't realise it yet.'

Lord, Jamie thought, are all Scotswomen fey or what?

'I expect you think I'm a conniving busybody,' Mrs McKay said with a rusty chuckle, and Jamie smiled, tears in her eyes.

'I think no such thing,' she said huskily. 'I'll treasure it, wedding or no wedding. Thank you.'

She laid a gentle kiss against the soft, wrinkled cheek, and straightened. 'Now, let's have a look at you.'

Mrs McKay stilled her hand. 'There's no need, lass. I know as well as you that it's all over.' She squeezed Jamie's hand, and then said quietly, 'I don't suppose Dr Buchanan could pop over? I just wanted to thank him—he's been so good to me these last few years. He puts me in mind of my husband as a young man—tall and strong, full of life and laughter. We had such fun, my Rabbie and I. It'll be good to see him again.'

Jamie got to her feet. 'I'll ring him,' she said, and dialled the number from the phone in the kitchen.

'Buchanan,' he said abruptly.

'Rob, I'm with Mrs McKay. She wondered if you could pop over.'

'What, now? But you're there.'

'Yes, but she wants to see you. Are you busy?'

'No, not really. I was having a go at the paperwork. Why?'

'Because I think you should come now.'

There was a silence, and he said quietly, 'Is she going?'

'I think so.'

'I'll be with you in fifteen minutes,' he said, and the line went dead.

She went slowly back into the sitting-room. 'He's coming. He'll be here in a few minutes.'

'Thank you, lassie,' she said softly, and her eyes closed. She slipped easily into sleep, and Jamie watched her chest rise and fall as she waited for the sound of Rob's Land Rover on the road.

He was there in just over ten minutes, and she opened the front door just as he pulled up.

'She's asleep,' Jamie told him, and he nodded.

She followed him back in, and he crouched beside the settee and held her hand.

'Mrs McKay? Annie? It's me—Rob Buchanan.'

Her lids flickered up, and she focused slowly on his face. 'Doctor—sorry, I must have dropped off.'

He smiled. 'Don't worry. Dr Cameron said you wanted to see me.'

'Oh, yes. . . I wanted to thank you, Dr Buchanan.

You've been so good to me—done far more than was needed. And I wanted to ask you one last favour.'

'Ask away,' he said huskily.

'Would you look after my cat? The black and white one—Charlie, the wee scamp's called. The others are half wild, but him—he'll miss me, and I'd like to think he went tae a good home.'

On cue the cat leapt on to her legs and rubbed against Rob's shoulder. He scratched its ears and it purred contentedly.

'Coming to live with me, then, old chap?' Rob crooned, and the cat made a funny chirruping sound and rubbed against him again.

'There, he knows,' she said with satisfaction.

'Mrs McKay, won't you let me ring your family and get you into hospital?' Rob asked her quietly, but she shook her head.

'There's nae point—the family will only fuss, and the hospital. . . I wish I could see my garden—is the sun shining?'

'Aye, it's warm and sunny now. Let me wrap you in a rug and I'll take you out.'

'Can you manage?'

He grinned at her. 'A wee slip of a lass like yoursel'? I should imagine so!'

He picked up an eiderdown off the chair and wrapped her in it, swinging her up into his arms as easily as if she were Chloe.

Jamie opened the back door, and then followed them as Rob wandered round the garden, pointing out the flowers to Mrs McKay.

'Och, look, the weeds! Rabbie'll be cross wi'me for neglecting it.'

'Nonsense. Ten minutes out here'll have it cleared.'

There was a bench by the roses, and Rob eased himself down, Mrs McKay cradled tenderly against his chest, while Jamie tugged up some of the larger weeds. Mrs McKay watched her and nodded with satisfaction.

'This is a lovely rose, Mrs McKay,' Jamie said, burying her nose in one of the deep velvet blooms.

'My Rabbie planted that rose,' she said contentedly. 'It was the year our Gordon got married—he died the next year, Rabbie did—just dropped down dead in the middle of his tea. I always said he'd do anything t'avoid the washing up!'

Rob laughed, his chest rumbling under the old lady's ear, and she laid her head against it and rested her hand over his heart.

Jamie picked one of the deep red roses and tucked it into Mrs McKay's hand. She sniffed deeply, and sighed.

'"O, my Luve's like a red red rose That's newly sprung in June"—always was my favourite,' she murmured, and then she seemed to doze off for a moment. When she woke, she pressed her hand to Rob's heart and smiled.

'They told me you were deid, Rabbie,' she whispered, 'but I didnae believe 'em. See, I can feel your heart beat. "And I will luve thee still, my dear"—cannae remember the rest,' she said fretfully.

'"Till a' the seas run dry,"' Rob finished, his voice gravelly. He leant forwards and pressed his lips to her forehead. 'Go to sleep now, Annie,' he murmured.

'Aye,' she whispered, her voice almost gone. 'I love you, Rabbie.'

Then she was quiet, and gradually the red rose slipped from her fingers.

'She's gone, Rob,' Jamie said gently.

He looked at her, his eyes glazed with tears, and nodded. 'Aye, I know. Would you call her son Gordon? His number's in the phone book. I'll stay here with her for a minute.'

She made her way into the house, her eyes misted with tears, and rang Gordon McKay and the undertakers. Then she went into the sitting-room and perched on the edge of the chair. The patchwork was on the arm, and she picked it up and held it against her chest and told herself firmly that the old lady was better off, that she was lonely and unwell and that she had had a good life, but it didn't work. She went back to the kitchen and stood in the doorway watching Rob.

She could hear him singing 'Auld Lang Syne' very softly, and then he got to his feet and carried Mrs McKay back in. Jamie stood back to let him pass, and then followed him through to the sitting-room. He laid her gently on the settee and covered her up, then tucked the red rose into her hair.

'Just do me a favour, eh?' he said gruffly to Jamie, his accent more pronounced than ever. 'Don't patronise me by telling me I shouldnae ha' got so involved.'

'Who, me?' she said with a choked little laugh, 'I wouldn't dream of it,' and then she was in his arms, and he was hugging all the air out of her lungs.

And then abruptly she was free, and he was all business again, examining the frail body and writing out the death certificate. He signed it, the undertakers arrived and took her body away, and they were left standing in the empty cottage.

'What's that?' he asked, and she realised she was still clutching the patchwork under her arm.

'She gave it to me—it's not quite finished, but she said there wasn't time——'

She broke off and turned away, and the cat came and wound himself round her ankles. She picked him up and handed him to Rob. 'Yours, I believe.'

He gave a sighing chuckle. 'I believe so. Come on, Charlie, let's go home.'

They locked up the cottage and then Jamie followed Rob back to the empty house.

He waited for her at the front door, and suggested she go in and get a firm hold of Bess—'Just in case they take a violent dislike to each other!'

She went into the kitchen, took Bess firmly by the collar, and told her that she was to be good and quiet and not make a fuss. Then Rob walked in and put the cat down, and they both held their breath.

Charlie miaowed indignantly, stalked over to the stove, sat down and washed himself thoroughly from end to end. After a cursory glance Bess ignored him, tail thrashing, and whined at Rob.

'Let her go,' he suggested, and she dashed over to him and licked his hand vigorously. 'That's that problem sorted out,' he said with a weary smile, and after he had washed his hands he filled the kettle. 'Tea, I think—did you get lunch?'

She shook her head. Lunchtime seemed so long ago. 'Did you?'

'Yes, Mrs H sat me down and force-fed me. There's some salad in the fridge if you want it, or we can have supper as soon as I've done the evening surgery—there's a casserole that just needs reheating in the oven, and a cold apple pie in the larder.'

'Sounds great.'

They drank their tea in companionable silence, and then Jamie took her patchwork upstairs and put it in a drawer until she had time to finish it. While Rob took surgery, she had a long soak in the bath, and then he ran up and showered while she dished up. They had supper at seven in the kitchen with Bess and the puppy and Charlie all looking on with interest.

'Quite a menagerie,' he said drily.

'For someone who doesn't like pets, yes,' she said with a smile.

'Who said I don't like pets? I just think they need time, and that, frankly, I don't have much of.'

She laughed. 'Tell me about it. We can't even have a conversation without being interrupted!'

Just then the doorbell rang, and Rob stood up and went out into the hall.

'Gordon—come in. I'm sorry about your mother.'

Lord, Jamie thought, Gordon McKay, and quickly cleared the table, stacking the plates in the sink and putting the kettle on.

He stayed for half an hour, had a cup of coffee and then left. After he'd gone Jamie made a fresh pot of coffee and took it into the sitting-room.

Rob joined her and sank down into the settee with a sigh.

'Sit next to me,' he said wearily, and lifted his arm

so she could snuggle up to his side. After a time, he shook his head and picked up his cup.

'Funny how he couldn't accept that she could just have died of old age. "But what was wrong with her?" he kept saying. "How could she just have stopped? There must have been something—a heart attack or something." Just couldn't accept that she was worn out and ready to stop.'

'How old was she?' Jamie asked.

'Eighty-five. Ready to go.'

'And a lovely way to die, so peaceful. But you'll miss her.'

'Och, aye. She was a rare character, and I've seen a lot of her, especially recently. That's the thing about grief, though, isn't it? It is a selfish emotion, and we're brought up not to be selfish, so we don't feel we have a right to grieve. That's why so many people have such a hard time, because they deny themselves what they consider to be self-indulgence. They don't realise it's all part of the healing process.'

Jamie nodded. It all made perfect sense to her. When her mother had died, she felt she had to be strong for her father, and so she had hidden her feelings for years. Now, with her father's death, somehow there hadn't been time—until Rob had made time for her last weekend. Since then she had allowed and accepted the sadness, shedding in private the much needed tears, and now she could feel the wound healing.

Thanks to him. She put down her cup and snuggled closer, resting her hand over his heart as Mrs McKay had done. 'You were very sweet to her in the garden,' she said softly.

'Och—that's why I'm a GP. Can you imagine picking up a hospital patient and carrying her out into the garden to die?'

His voice cracked on the last word, and she reached up and cradled his cheek, pulling his head down to kiss away the lines of pain that were etched on his craggy cheeks.

'Ah, love. . .' He tilted her head and brushed his lips across her mouth, his touch feather-light, his hand threading through her hair and cupping her head to steady her. The other hand lay warm against her hip, and the warmth seemed to radiate out from it to reach every part of her.

Her lips parted on a sigh, and with a muffled groan he deepened the kiss. The fires which had raged beneath the surface all week broke free, and suddenly she was as eager as Rob, her hands trembling on the buttons of his shirt.

'Damn,' she said tremulously, 'I want to touch you, but these buttons——'

He wrenched the shirt open, tearing off the buttons, and her hands fell on his chest, alive to the crisp texture of the black hair that sprang in curls over the front of his chest. Her hands slid round to the sides, marvelling at the change to smooth, silken skin overlying the powerful muscles of his back and shoulders.

She could feel his hands trembling against her spine through the thin silk of her shirt, and she ached for his touch on her bare skin, to feel his hands on her as her hands were on him.

'Damn clothes,' he said raggedly, as if he could read her mind. 'Jamie?'

'Yes,' she told him, her eyes expressing more clearly than words her need for him.

'Come on,' he murmured, his voice husky. He rose to his feet and held out his hand palm up, and she laid hers trustingly in it and let him lead her towards the stairs.

Her heart was pounding, her bones turned to jelly, and she stumbled on the first step.

'OK?'

'I——' Her eyes wide, she stared helplessly at him. 'My legs don't seem too good——'

He swept her up into his arms and carried her easily up the rest of the stairs to his room, kicking the door shut behind him with his foot. Then he lowered her carefully to her feet, and stepped back.

'Are you sure?' he said gruffly. His eyes were heavy with desire but still he found time to be concerned for her.

'Quite sure,' she breathed, and his eyes closed with relief.

Then there was no more need for words as he led her gently to the bed and undressed her, his eyes lingering on her body as it was revealed to him.

Finally she stood before him wearing only the cream silk teddy he had teased her with the first time he had kissed her. How long ago that seemed, how strange that she should have felt such shame. Now her reaction to him seemed so natural and right.

She felt no shyness, no sense of false modesty or shame, only a glorious awareness of her womanhood as Rob gazed at her. His chest was rising and falling in time with his harsh breathing, and in the hollow of his throat she could see a pulse beating rapidly.

He swallowed and lifted his eyes to hers. 'You're wearing it—God, Jamie, I have had such fantasies. . .'

Slowly, never taking his eyes off hers for a second, he kicked off his shoes and shrugged off the tattered remains of his shirt, then hooking his thumbs in the waistband of his trousers, he stripped off the rest of his clothes in one.

Her breath caught in her throat, her heart so full that she was unable to speak. He was magnificent, so beautiful—and he wanted her. Her, Jamie, the last twenty-nine year old virgin in the world. Suddenly assailed by doubts, she shut her eyes and bit her lip. What if Martin was right? What if she failed to satisfy him?

His hands were gentle, easing her body up against his, stroking and soothing as he murmured softly to her.

'Touch me,' he whispered.

And then suddenly it was all right, because the fire was back and she met him kiss for kiss, touch for touch.

He picked her up and laid her on the bed, easing his weight down beside her, and then, with infinite gentleness and care, he made her his.

She cried out with a mixture of pain and ecstasy, and he stilled, lifting his head to stare down at her, his eyes shocked and puzzled.

'Jamie?'

'Please, Rob!' she begged, her hands reaching up to clutch feverishly at his back.

'Oh, sweetheart. . .' His lips came down to meet

hers, so gentle, so tender, but her passion soared and she clung to him, soft cries of desire rising up in her throat and inflaming him until she felt his control shatter just as the waves of passion broke within her.

He cried out and clung to her, his body shuddering in release, and she held him close, murmuring soft words of love through her tears.

When his breathing slowed he lifted his head and gazed down at her.

'Are you all right?' he murmured. 'You didn't tell me. . .'

She nodded, too moved to speak, and he eased his weight off her and tucked her close into his side, her head cradled on his chest, his arms wrapped closely round her, his hand stroking idly up and down her spine.

His heart beat steadily under her ear, and she lay her hand on his deep chest and threaded her fingers into the soft curls.

'Rob?' she whispered.

'Mmm?'

'I love you.'

He went still, his body tensed as if alert to danger, then gradually he relaxed and his hand moved again against her spine. He pressed his lips against her hair, and his arms tightened about her.

'You're getting cold,' he murmured huskily, and tugged the quilt over them both, tucking it in round her shoulders.

Was he going to ignore her? For weeks she had held back the words, waiting for a time when it would be right to tell him of her feelings. Surely to God there couldn't be a better time than now? Hot tears spilt from her eyes and cascaded on to his chest, and he rolled her over, his face serious.

'Ah, love, don't. . .' he whispered, and kissed away the tears, his lips warm and soft, tender on her skin.

In the face of his gentleness her panic faded, and she gave herself over to the subtle beauty of his love-making. Surely, she told herself, surely if he could touch her like this, with such care, such infinite sweetness, then he must return her love.

He must. . .

CHAPTER NINE

ON FRIDAY night Jamie had discovered that passion had heights she had never dreamt of. On Saturday and Sunday she discovered its depths and breadths. Rob was wonderful with her—totally frank, generous to a fault and often funny. She had never associated sex with humour, but again and again she found herself helpless with laughter—and then with a touch of his hand, a brush of his lips, she was scaling the heights again.

She held her tongue, though. No more confessions of love, although her heart ached to open to him and she shed bitter-sweet tears every time he made love to her.

They walked on the heather with Bess, played with the puppy, turned the cat off Rob's bed over and over again, and then on Sunday afternoon she gathered up all her things that had somehow percolated through into his room and went back to propriety.

Mrs Harrison had had a wonderful weekend and regaled them with tales of the wedding. They listened with polite enthusiasm, their eyes meeting periodically across the room to mourn the passing of their precious time together.

On Monday afternoon Chloe came back, and Rob welcomed her with open arms and obvious love. Ridiculous, to be jealous of his child, but her heart ached and she took herself off so she didn't have to watch them together.

She heard his footsteps on the landing after he had put Chloe to bed, and with a brief knock he slipped through her door and shut it behind him.

'I missed you last night,' he said with a rueful smile.

'I missed you, too,' she murmured. 'It seemed a very long, cold night.'

He opened his arms and she burrowed against his chest, hugging him tight.

'I'm not sure I can stand sneaking around my own home in the middle of the night, but I'm not about to offend Mrs H's sensibilities by suggesting you sleep with me openly.'

She squeezed him affectionately. 'Don't worry. There'll be times when we're alone.'

He tilted her chin and kissed her, and then released her with a sigh.

'Come and have a coffee with me. You're on call, and it was a quiet weekend so I expect all hell will break loose shortly.'

Too right, she thought later as she let herself back in at two-thirty. She hadn't had time to finish that cup of coffee, or the next one.

'Why did I want to be a GP?' she muttered to herself as she slipped off her shoes and tiptoed up the stairs. The house was silent except for the ticking of the clock in the hall, and she looked longingly at Rob's bedroom door on the way past. Oh, to slip into bed beside him and snuggle into the warmth of his arms!

That was what she missed the most, she decided, the human contact, the feeling of being cherished. He might not be able to tell her that he loved her, might not want to hear it from her, but he was a long way from being indifferent. It was almost as if he didn't trust the strength of her emotions.

She was called out again on Tuesday morning at six, and came back to find him sitting at the kitchen table reading a journal over a cup of tea.

'Hi,' she said softly, and bent to kiss him.

'Hi. Lousy night—I'm sorry.'

She smiled. 'Swings and roundabouts. I'm glad it happened last night and not at the weekend.'

He met her eyes, his own blazing, and her heart kicked into overdrive.

'Me, too. What's that?' He nodded towards her hand.

'Oh, I forgot, I met the postman,' she said breathlessly, and handed him a pile of letters.

He flicked through them, and then his hands stilled.

'What the hell now?' he muttered under his breath.

Jamie watched him anxiously as he ripped open the official-looking white envelope and scanned the contents.

The colour drained from his face and his hands shook.

'She can't!' he whispered harshly. 'No! I won't let her!'

'Who? What? Rob, talk to me—what is it?'

He lifted his eyes to her and looked at her as if he had never seen her before.

'Rob?'

His hand tightened on the letter and he screwed it

into a ball. 'That bitch—she's married again and she wants Chloe back!'

Jamie sat down abruptly and took the letter out of his hand. She smoothed it out and read it through, then read it again, and then looked up at him, her eyes huge with anguish.

'I thought you had custody?'

'I never bothered—she didn't want her, I had no reason to believe she would pull a stunt like this—what the hell can I do? Jamie, I can't lose her, I'll die without her, I love her. And she needs me. She's never known her mother—she'll be miserable without me—oh, God, what do I do?'

'There's only one thing you can do—you'll have to fight for her. You're bound to win, you've raised her from birth!'

He laughed bitterly. 'Oh, yes—the hours I work, and I'm on my own—if I was married it might be different, but I'm not, and the courts have no logic in these cases. When it comes to custody the mother always wins hands down.'

'Not always,' Jamie told him. 'Surely each case is measured on its merits?'

'Oh, yes, and what are the merits in my case? She's well fed and cared for, but I'm often out, I work ridiculous hours, and she spends all her time in the company of a middle-aged woman. I'll fail, and they'll take her from me, for the same reasons they won't let me have Trudy if the need arises—she's a girl, I'm a single man, and as far as the court's concerned that'll probably be enough!'

'So get married.'

Her words dropped like stones into the silence of the kitchen.

'Don't be absurd,' he said eventually.

'I wasn't.'

He snorted. 'Of course you were! Quite apart from the fact that I live out here in the back of beyond, I'm no oil-painting, Jamie. It's easy to say, but who the hell would have me?'

She met his eyes with all the love she could muster, her heart pounding in her throat. 'I would,' she said honestly.

He stared at her in disbelief. 'Don't be daft, woman. Why the hell would you want to do a damn fool thing like that?'

'Because I love you?'

There, she had said it. Not in a moment of passion, but calmly, logically, and from the heart. For a moment hope flickered in his eyes, but then it was gone.

'No,' he said flatly. 'You think you love me, because like all women you have to sanitise your sexual feelings by endowing them with romance. You don't love me any more than I love you, and even if you did I couldn't condemn you to a life in this backwater. It would be a disaster, and then we'd all end up back at square one again.'

'But why should it be a disaster?'

He sighed impatiently. 'Because happy ever after doesn't exist, Jamie.'

'What about Mrs McKay? She was still in love with her husband the day she died!'

'That's exceptional. A love like that is very rare——'

'But you agree it can exist?'

'Not for me, Jamie—not for us. I appreciate what you're trying to do for me and Chloe—thank you for the gesture, but no—I'll fight this on my own.'

She forced herself to meet his gaze squarely, despite the pain raging inside her.

'And if you lose?'

'I won't,' he said harshly. 'I can't afford to. Will you take the branch surgery for me this morning? I need to ring my solicitor.'

'Of course,' she said heavily.

He went out and left her there, swamped by rage and sorrow, her heart breaking not only for herself, but for him and for Chloe, still lying asleep upstairs, totally unaware of the upheaval waiting for her just around the corner.

When she came back from Glenlivie, Mrs Harrison was alone in the kitchen, her eyes red-rimmed and her mouth tight, venting her spleen on a lump of unsuspecting bread dough. 'Scheming witch,' she muttered with a thump. 'What does she want the bairn for anyway? Only to punish him, though what he's ever done to her I should like to know.'

She pummelled her fists into the dough, and Jamie laid a hand on her wrist and squeezed gently.

'That won't be fit to eat in a moment,' she said gently, and Mrs Harrison's head fell forward with a little sob.

'Damn her,' she wept, and Jamie hugged her shaking shoulders comfortingly, and led her to a chair.

'Let me make you a cup of tea,' she said soothingly. 'Where's Rob?'

'In the surgery, on the phone again to his solicitor. Chloe's having a lie down. I think the weekend tired her out.'

She sniffed and blew her nose loudly, then blotted her tear-stained cheeks.

'He's a damn fool, of course,' she said fondly, 'if he would only marry you, it would solve all his problems.'

'I've already offered,' Jamie said with a sigh, putting two cups of tea down on the table and dropping miserably into a chair.

'And?'

'He turned me down.'

'Well, then, he's an even bigger fool than I thought. I suppose he tried the usual bit about living in the middle of nowhere?'

Jamie nodded.

'Sometimes I wonder if he's using it as an excuse so he doesn't have to try again,' Mrs Harrison said sagely. 'The way he looks at you, lass—especially since the weekend.'

Jamie flushed scarlet, and Mrs Harrison patted her hand.

'I'm not blind, pet. You're adults; it's up to you what you do. But I can't help feeling you're both hurting now.'

'He doesn't believe I love him,' Jamie said brokenly. 'That woman's destroyed his trust in love, and now she's trying to finish him off. How can she be so cruel? Doesn't she care at all?'

'Only for herself.' Mrs Harrison drained her tea and stood up, then lifted her hand to her head.

'Are you OK?' Jamie asked her.

'Aye, I think so. Busy weekend, and now all this—I've just got a bit of a headache, that's all.'

'Why don't you go and lie down? I'll get us some lunch and then look after Chloe—I'm off all afternon. I'll take her out for a walk with Bess later if the weather clears up.'

Mrs Harrison shot her a grateful look. 'If you're sure, lass?'

'Of course I'm sure. Go on, go and have a rest.'

She prepared a light salad for lunch, and then went into Rob's surgery to find him.

He was standing at the window, his shoulders hunched, his hands jammed into the pockets of his trousers. His face was racked with anguish.

'Rob? What did he say?'

He shut his eyes and she saw a muscle working in his jaw.

She reached out and laid a hand on his arm, and she was shocked at the tension in him. He was rigid, his body coiled like a spring.

'Rob? Darling, what did he say?'

He drew in a harsh breath and stared down the rain-lashed garden. 'She's got a fifty-fifty chance.'

She was shocked. 'As much as that?' she gasped.

'Oh, aye—unless I'm married! Then she stands practically no chance.' He gave a bitter grunt of laughter. 'Mrs Harrison's had a go at me on the subject as well. Frankly I wish you'd all mind your own damn business!'

He turned away from her, his shoulders ramrod straight.

Ignoring the stabbing pain in the region of her heart, Jamie reached out to him again.

'It's only because we care about you,' she said unevenly.

'I'm sorry,' he admitted gruffly. 'I don't mean to hurt you, but I just don't know which way to turn.'

'Come and have some lunch,' she urged gently.

'I don't want any——'

'Rob you have to eat——'

'I said, I don't want any! Damn it, Jamie, just leave me alone!'

Bitterly hurt, she turned on her heel and walked out, closing the door quietly behind her. Perhaps later he would be in a more reasonable frame of mind, she told herself, and stifled the sob that rose in her throat.

He went out shortly afterwards, and she chased the salad round her plate for a few minutes before acknowledging that she, too, didn't want to eat.

She took her coffee into the sitting-room and sat staring morosely down the garden. If he would only trust her, accept her love. . .

Over her head Chloe began to sing to her teddy, and, with a weary sigh, Jamie went up and changed her nappy and brought the little girl downstairs. She grilled her some fish fingers and chopped some salad, and then, when she had finished and smeared a yoghurt all over her face, Jamie cleaned her up and took her back into the little sitting-room.

They played happily with her toys for a while, and Jamie sang to her, sitting her on her foot and bouncing her up and down. She sang 'The Grand Old Duke of York', and when she got to the 'up', she lifted her leg up and held Chloe in the air, giggling and shrieking, "gain!'

She did it again, and, just as she swung her leg up, Rob walked into the room. They didn't see him, and when the verse was finished Jamie scooped Chloe into her arms, laughing, and hugging her tight.

'Was that fun?' she asked.

The little dark curls bounced affirmative.

'Want to do it again?'

Chloe looked up at that moment and saw Rob, standing transfixed in the doorway, his face rigid with anger.

'Daddy do it!' she squealed, and, wriggling off Jamie's lap, she ran to him and held up her arms. He swung her easily up on to his hip and glowered at Jamie.

'I've warned you, Jamie. Leave my daughter alone! There's enough heartbreak lined up without you adding to it—where's Mrs H?'

She swallowed her anger for Chloe's sake, and tried to answer him calmly. 'She had a headache—I told her to lie down.'

'How convenient,' he sneered.

'As it happens, it was. I wasn't doing anything else this afternoon, so she was able to go and rest. You forget, she's under a lot of strain too.'

'She should have said something——'

'What, and add to your problems? Don't be silly. Anyway, don't you think you're making rather a lot of this?'

'In the circumstances, no, I don't. She's mine, Jamie, and nobody's going to take her away from me.'

'Daddy, stop shouting!' Chloe told him firmly, and pressed her chubby hand over his mouth.

He kissed it, and Jamie saw his eyes blur with tears. 'Sorry, sweetheart. I'm just a bit tired.'

'Poor Daddy,' Chloe murmured, and snuggled into his side, tucking her thumb in her mouth.

He shut his eyes and drew a deep breath, then eased himself down into a chair, Chloe on his lap.

'Shall we read a story?' he suggested.

Just then the phone rang, and Jamie stood up swiftly and went to answer it.

It was Sandy Reeve. Apparently Josie had developed a temperature and a sore breast, and probably had mastitis.

She stuck her head back round the sitting room door. 'Josie Reeve, query mastitis. I'll go.'

His face was anguished. 'But you're off duty.'

'So what do you suggest?'

He closed his eyes and his mouth tightened with the internal battle he was waging.

'As I see it, you and Chloe need each other. So, I'll go—I'm sorry if that screws up any preconceived notion you might have had about me worming my way into her affections, but that's just tough. You can show your gratitude by finding a locum—I'm leaving!'

She slammed out of the house, got into her car and then groaned. The Reeves' house was right at the end of that awful track—climbing out of the car, she went back into the sitting-room and held out her hand.

'I'll need the keys of the Land Rover,' she said tersely.

'Jamie, don't do this to me now!'

'Why not? I refuse to stay here and become the whipping post for all your emotional hang-ups, or some kind of sexual convenience to take to bed when things get a little boring round here! Give me the keys!'

'You don't understand——'

'Too damn right I don't understand! I don't understand how you can be so blind to your own feelings as well as everybody else's. I'll see you later. I suggest you use the time phoning the locum agency. Now give me the damn keys!'

He slapped them into her hand, and she marched out again, head held high. Her pride kept her going until she was halfway to the Reeves before she had to pull over and give in to her tears.

Finally she blotted her face dry, patted on some make-up to cover the ravages and drove the rest of the way to the cottage.

Josie was lying on the settee, her colour a little high, and she was obviously relieved to see Jamie.

'I'm glad it's you,' she confessed. 'Somehow, now all the business of the birth is over, I hate the thought of undressing in front of a man again!'

Jamie smiled. 'Let's have a look at you, then. All your stitches out OK?'

Josie nodded. 'No problem—I feel a bit tender still, but much better than I did.'

'So tell me about this,' Jamie said, as Josie undressed and showed her the tender area under her right breast. 'When did it start?'

'It's been sore for a few days—since Saturday, maybe? Not much, but getting worse, and today I had a temperature and it was very sore—I can't wear my bra.'

'No, well, I wouldn't, not for a day or two. It may have been caused by the pressure of your bra against the engorged tissue—you've got quite a lot of milk, haven't you? You need to encourage the baby to drink from this breast first, to relieve the pressure, and then switch after the first five or ten minutes—don't give him too long, or you'll start to produce more milk on this side and it'll feel worse! I'll give you some antibiotics and you can take paracetamol, up to eight a day, quite safely. Don't take more than that, and ring if it doesn't show a marked improvement in twenty-four hours. OK? The midwife'll keep an eye on it for you and tell you if you need to see one of us again.'

With a smile at Sandy and the baby, she drove back to Glencorran. By the time she got back Mrs Harrison was up and Rob was in his surgery.

'He wants to see you, lass,' Mrs Harrison told her. 'Here, I've just made a cup of tea for him. I'll pour you one, too—there, take them with you.'

She handed Jamie the tray and bustled back into the kitchen.

Taking a deep, steadying breath, Jamie knocked on Rob's door and went in.

He was sitting at the desk, his head bowed, his hands hanging between his knees. He looked the picture of despair, and Jamie wished yet again that he would let her help him. But he wouldn't, she knew that, and the only way to keep her sanity was to get as far away from him as she could. Perhaps the Sudan?

He lifted his head then, and gave her a weary smile.

'I've brought you some tea.'

'Thanks. Jamie, I'm sorry—I don't know why I'm such a bastard.'

'I'm sorry, too. Really, Rob, this afternoon with Chloe I was only trying to give Mrs H a break——'

'I know that. I just over-reacted when I saw her having fun with you. I'm trying to tell myself she'll be miserable if she ends up with Jennifer, but there's no guarantee she will, of course. She seemed quite happy with you——'

'Here, in her own home, with you around most of the time. Don't forget that. And if she's happy with other people and doesn't cling to you, it's all credit to you for the way you've brought her up to be so happy and confident. She's very well-adjusted, Rob. Surely the court will see that? You won't lose her, don't worry.'

'And you? Will I lose you?'

She dropped her eyes. 'I think it's probably for the best, don't you? If you can't believe in me, and you're worried about me hurting Chloe, then perhaps I should go, and the sooner the better.'

'I've found a locum—he can start after next week, if you're sure?'

She nodded blindly.

'Where will you go?'

'I—I don't know. Friends, I expect. . .' Suddenly her eyes filled with tears. 'I'll find something, Rob, don't worry. Perhaps some nice little town in the Home

Counties where I won't have to worry about getting snowed in or lost——'

She broke off and busied herself with her tea.

'I didn't mean to hurt you,' he said gently.

She sniffed. 'I know. Listen, about Josie Reeve—she's got mastitis in her right breast. I've given her antiobiotics and told her to keep an eye on it. She seems to be doing OK.'

'Good. Thanks. Jamie, will you be all right?'

'I expect so. What the hell are you going to do about it if I'm not?' she snapped miserably, and, dumping her tea back on the tray, she ran out of his surgery and up to her room.

She half expected him to come after her, but then she heard the front door close and the Land Rover started, and she realised he was going out on call. Crossing to the window, she watched him drive away until the tears blinded her. Then she crawled under the covers of her bed and cried until she thought her heart would break.

CHAPTER TEN

THE next few days were fraught with emotion and difficulty, but they were nothing compared to the weekend.

Rob had been morose and uncommunicative all week, and Jamie found it hard to reconcile this man with the tender and considerate lover of the weekend.

Gone were the sizzling glances, the stolen kisses and caresses, the comforting hugs. In their place was a distance ravaged by emotional conflict that Jamie found hard to bear.

She was on call this weekend, and Mrs Harrison was technically off duty, although she wasn't going away. Jamie hoped that Rob would take Chloe down to his parents in Oban for the weekend, as he had before, but he announced over breakfast that he was going to try and tackle the other downstairs room to rearrange the waiting areas.

But the best laid plans and all that. While Jamie was still trying to absorb the information that he would be here all weekend, the phone rang.

As she was on call she answered it, to find that it was Mrs Douglas. 'Is Dr Buchanan there?' she asked anxiously.

'Yes, he is, Mrs Douglas, but I'm on call. Can I help?'

'Oh—oh, well—it's Trudy. They've called to say

they've got a kidney for her, and I don't know what to do!'

'Oh, that's wonderful! Hang on, I'll get him——'

She turned and bumped straight into him. 'Mrs Douglas,' she said breathlessly. 'They've got a kidney for Trudy.'

'Thank God, and about time—Mrs Douglas! Hello. Yes, she told me. It's marvellous news. Aye, of course I will—wouldn't miss it for the world. Throw some things in a bag, I'll be with you in a few minutes.'

He put the phone down and grinned at Jamie. 'Can you manage if I go to Inverness with them? They need transport, and I want to be there—I just feel. . . Do you mind if I go?'

'You don't have to explain to me, Rob. Of course I can manage, and of course you must go. Give Trudy my love and a big hug. Take my car—here, you'll need the keys. Can I have the Land Rover?'

They swapped keys, then he kissed Chloe goodbye and ran for the door. 'Tell Mrs H—I'm sure she won't mind covering for this!'

And then he was gone, the door banging shut behind him.

Chloe peered up at Jamie and frowned.

'Daddy gone?'

'Yes, darling. Trudy's got to go to hospital, and he's going to take her. He'll be back later today.' She scooped the little girl up and carried her back into the kitchen. 'Want to help me feed the puppy?'

Between the three of them, they got through the day, Jamie and Mrs Harrison sharing Chloe whenever Jamie wasn't out on a call.

They put her to bed at seven, and by ten Jamie was beginning to worry about Rob.

'You go to bed,' she told Mrs Harrison. 'I'll wait up for him.'

She had a shower and put on her jogging suit, then sat in the chair in the sitting-room, legs curled up under her bottom and a book on her lap—not that she could concentrate on reading it for the thoughts whirling in her head.

She wondered how Trudy was—whether the match had been considered good enough, whether the operation had been a success, if the graft kidney would be rejected—all questions which would be answered in time, she knew, but still she worried.

And she also spared a thought for the relatives of the donor. How were they feeling at this moment? Were they deriving any comfort from knowing that their loved one would benefit several other people through the medium of transplant surgery?

Like most members of the medical profession, Jamie carried a donor card, but she wondered how she would feel if Rob died and his organs were donated. Would it be a comfort? Or would the tragedy of his death so overwhelm her that the concept of benefiting others was too remote?

She glanced again at her watch. Eleven forty-two. She tried to work out the times again. If he had picked up the Douglases at eight, he would be in Inverness by ten-thirty. Cross-matching and tissue-type check would take a few hours—say four—that was two-thirty. Probably three o'clock. Then prepping up, the operation, recovery—probably another six hours. That was nine.

Three hours back—midnight. If he stayed to see Trudy after the operation, that might delay him another hour.

One o'clock, then, before she needed to worry.

There was nothing interesting on the television, so she made a cup of coffee to help keep herself awake and settled down to read the newspaper.

She must have dozed off, because, the next thing she knew, Rob was squatting down in front of her, his face lined with strain, shaking her gently awake.

'Jamie—wake up, love. I'm back.'

'Rob. . .' She straightened stiffly, and eased her cramped legs out from underneath her. 'How's Trudy? How did it go?'

'Fine—she's fine. The operation appears to have been a success. The donor kidney started producing urine as soon as they connected it up to the blood supply, and there was a steady stream through the catheter by the time I left. They took hours cross-matching—Mrs Douglas nearly collapsed with the strain, but Trudy was wonderful. She's such a gutsy little kid. Then they came and gave us the green light, and that was it.'

'Did you stay with Mrs Douglas?'

'Part of the time. I spent about an hour in the viewing gallery watching the operation. I hadn't realised how tiny she is until I saw them working on her——'

His voice cracked, and he shook his head. 'Sorry, it's been a hell of a day.'

'It's been a hell of a week,' she corrected, and had to fight the urge to brush the hair back off his brow.

He, however, had no such inhibitions. He laid his

head on her lap and sighed. 'It's good to be home,' he mumbled. 'How's Chloe?'

'Fine. We went for a walk with Bess and fed the seagulls, and Mrs H made some buns with her this afternoon and she decorated them—you have to see them, they're in the kitchen. Not wildly successful, but she had a lot of fun. Can I get you anything to eat or drink?'

'No, I'm too tired—perhaps a drink? I couldn't eat anything.'

'You ought to try—how about a piece of toast?'

'OK—I'll just go up and see Chloe, and have a quick shower. I'll be down in a tick.' He glanced at his watch then and shook his head as if to clear it. 'Is it really half-past one?'

'Probably—go and have your shower, and I'll sort you something out.'

She chivvied him out of the door, and watched with a lump in her throat as he made his way wearily up the stairs.

Ten minutes later he was back, dressed in his short towelling robe and nothing else, droplets of water clinging to the curls so tantalisingly visible in the V on his chest.

'Here.' She sat him down in front of a pile of hot buttered toast and a big mug of tea, and perched on the chair opposite, lacing her fingers together so she didn't reach over the table and trace the drops of water down his chest. . .

'How long will she be in hospital?'

'Three weeks, probably,' he mumbled round the toast. 'Just to make sure she's not rejecting. They're putting her on cyclosporin and prednisolone for the first three months or so, then they'll gradually drop the prednisolone and keep her on cyclosporin. Still, that's all in the future.'

'I wonder how she'll get on?' Jamie said wistfully. 'Will you write and tell me?'

He met her eyes, his face slightly shocked, as though he had forgotten she was going.

'Of course. She'll be able to write to you herself soon.'

'Did you give her my love?'

He nodded. 'She wants to know if you can go and see her next week. In fact I want to go some time, so perhaps I'll get Iain from the next practice to cover one day if he can so we can go together. What do you think?'

Lord, she thought, three hours there and three hours back alone with you is what I think. I don't know if I can survive it. 'Fine,' she told him, knowing as she said it that it would be far from fine.

The phone rang then, and she tore herself away from him and answered it in the office.

'I have to go out—Roddy McIver—he's cut his hand.'

'Probably on a bottle—do you want me to go? He's a difficult customer. When I went up about the dog I didn't like the look of him at all.'

'No,' she told him firmly. 'I'll be fine. You get to bed, you look all in.'

Resisting the urge to ruffle his hair, she let herself out quietly and climbed into the Land Rover. Knowing where the farm was, she didn't relish ruining her car.

Of course, had she been staying she would have changed it for a more suitable vehicle, perhaps an old Isuzu jeep or something like that, but as it was. . .

She let the clutch in and bounded off the drive, ground the gears and rattled off up the road. Really, the Land Rover was a heap, she thought, but until Rob found someone to invest money in the practice she didn't suppose he would have enough to spare for cars. She knew Jackie had made a great difference to his income by claiming all the clinic fees, night calls and so on to which he was entitled, but, even so, it made precious little difference to the overall picture. If only he would listen to her——

She flung the Land Rover round the sharp bend into Roddy McIver's drive, and bounced and rattled her way to the ramshackle little farmhouse at the end.

There was a light on in the kitchen, and she banged on the back door and waited. Eventually she heard feet shuffling across stone flags, and the door creaked open a fraction.

'Who's there?'

'Dr Cameron—you called me, Mr McIver.'

'No, ah want the doctor—not some damn woman.'

She stuck her foot in the door and pushed gently. 'Dr Buchanan is off duty,' she told him. 'I'm on call tonight. Now, are you going to let me in, or are you going to bleed to death here?'

He grunted, and opened the door grudgingly, shuffling away across the floor again to sit down by the range in an old rocker.

In the dim light, Jamie could see that he had a bloodstained rag wrapped around his left hand, and the room reeked of Scotch.

'How did you cut yourself?' she asked him, crossing over to where he sat and opening her bag.

'Fell in the scullery wi' a glass,' he mumbled.

Jamie wasn't surprised. She unwrapped the rag and winced. 'You've got a deep cut here, Mr McIver,' she told him. 'I'll have to put stitches in it. I'll just give you an injection to numb it, then we'll be in business.'

She poured some antiseptic on to a cotton swab and wiped the area thoroughly. He winced and tugged his hand, but she held it tight and carried on.

'Hell, lassie! Are y'sure you know what you're doing? Ah dinnae want nae bluidy raw recruit messing aboot wi' ma person!'

'Quite sure, Mr McIver—anyway, needlework is what women are best at, isn't it?' she said sweetly.

He snorted. 'Got tae have some damn uses, ah s'pose. Bugger all guid at anythin' else out o'bed!' He gave her a considering look. 'Gather you're shacked up wi' the young doctor,' he said with an evil leer.

'I'm his partner,' she said tightly.

'Aye, that's what ah said!' he cackled.

As she drew up the lignocaine she toyed with the temptation of dispensing with the anaesthetic, but discretion got the better of her.

As she injected his hand, she was conscious of his scrutiny.

'You're sure you're old enough?'

'Quite old enough, Mr McIver.'

He sniffed. 'O'course, you're the lassie what stole ma dog, aren't you?'

She got a handle on her temper with difficulty, and returned his look with a level one of her own. 'Your dog, Mr McIver? Oh, you mean the one I found lying in the road half starved and beaten? She's well now—gaining weight at last, and the one surviving puppy is making progress, thank you for asking. How's the hand? Numb yet?'

She prodded it with a finger, and he winced.

She gave him another couple of minutes, during which they watched each other distrustfully, and then she pulled another chair up and sat down, tore open the suture pack, pulled on some sterile gloves and laid out a sterile paper towel on her lap.

'Right, Mr McIver, let's get you sewn up.'

It took her some time to draw the edges of the wound together to her satisfaction, and he whimpered and fussed and cussed and generally got on her nerves with every stitch.

In the normal course of events she would have been much more reassuring and conciliatory, but the lateness of the hour, worry about Trudy, Rob and Chloe, and knowing how he had treated Bess, just drove compassion clean out of her mind. She was brisk, professional and efficient, and he hated it.

Finally she was done, and he eyed the result with distaste.

'Expect yon'll hurt like a bugger in the mornin',' he grumbled.

'I don't doubt it. I should be more careful next time if I were you. Come and have your stitches out a week on Monday. Good night, Mr McIver.'

She let herself out, took several lungfuls of fresh,

clean air and headed back to the Land Rover. The knowledge that she wouldn't be there when he came to have his stitches removed hit her like a brick wall, and she leant her head against the door for a moment until the pain receded. Then she climbed in, fought with the gearbox and headed back to Glencorran. A little while later she pulled up on the drive and went in with a heavy heart.

She wasn't really looking where she was going and gasped in astonishment when she walked into a rock-hard chest.

'Rob!'

His arms closed gently around her.

'Are you OK?'

'Yes, I'm fine—what are you doing still up?'

He gave her a wry smile. 'I didn't like the thought of you up there with that madman all on your own in the middle of the night.'

She grinned. 'He didn't like it either—he would much rather have had you. I don't think he trusted me at all, the disgusting old goat.'

She gave Rob a keen look. 'You look all in, Rob. Why don't you go to bed?'

He met her eyes, and the message was all too clear.

'I don't suppose you'd like to come with me,' he said gruffly.

Suddenly conscious of his body, she eased herself gently but firmly out of his arms. 'No, Rob,' she answered quietly. 'I won't be used as a security blanket.'

'That isn't——'

'No, Rob. I mean it. When you can treat me as an

equal, trust me when I say I love you, when you can return my love—ask me again. Now I'm going to get some sleep before that blasted phone rings again.'

Avoiding his eyes, she trailed wearily upstairs, desperately conscious of Rob behind her, his eyes following her. She could picture the look in them, the defeat, the worry, the need—why am I being so hard on him? she wondered. What harm could it do?

Her steps faltered, and she heard him start up the stairs behind her.

'Jamie?'

'Goodnight, Rob,' she said heavily, and let herself into her room, shutting the door firmly behind her before she could change her mind.

Iain was able to cover for them on Friday afternoon so they could go and visit Trudy. Rob went up on Tuesday, straight from the branch surgery, and reported that she was making excellent progress and they were very pleased with her. Her urine output was good, and she already looked stronger than she had before the operation.

'How's her mother bearing up?' Jamie asked.

'Oh, OK, I suppose. She's absolutely exhausted, but there's no way she'll leave Trudy's side. Actually I'm quite concerned about her, and I think the staff up there are, too. I just hope it doesn't prove all too much for her and trigger a relapse. That would be the bloody limit at the moment.'

Jamie eyed him worriedly. His face looked leaner, the angles more sharply defined, and his eyes were bruised and hollow. Obviously he wasn't sleeping, and equally obviously he wasn't going to, so long as Jennifer persisted in her custody claim.

Realising that he was unable to take any more, she had kept their own relationship very low key, avoiding any potential conflict by keeping out of his way as much as possible.

But it was killing her. This was her last week with him. On Saturday she would leave Glencorran for ever, and Rob and Chloe would become a cherished memory. It was too much to cope with, so she threw herself into her work and kept out of his way, in the vain hope that she could ease herself out of the habit of his company.

She might as well have tried to fly. Every time she heard his voice, or the firm tread on the stairs, every time she saw him bent over holding Chloe's hand and walking with her up the garden or bouncing her on his knee, her heart broke a little further.

On Friday she covered the Glencorran practice while Rob went to Glenlivie. For once it was a relatively small turn-out, and she had time after her calls to have a cup of coffee with Mrs Harrison and Chloe in the little sitting-room.

'You're off tomorrow, then?' Mrs Harrison said quietly.

She nodded. 'Yes, I have to go.'

'Och, lass, it's such a shame. . .'

Jamie pressed her hand to her mouth. 'Don't,' she choked. 'I can just about get through if I don't think about it.'

'He's a damn fool, really. I cannae see why he's being so stiff-necked and stubborn.'

Jamie gave a slightly hysterical little laugh. 'He was born that way, Mrs H. Nothing I say will change him.' She looked away, blinking back the tears that clogged her vision.

Just then the front door banged and his firm, heavy tread marched down the hall.

'Jamie? You here? We have to go—ah, here you all are. Hello, sweetheart! Got a kiss for your daddy?'

Jamie leapt to her feet and hurried out, unable to watch the open exchange of affection between the two people she loved most in the world.

'I'll just get ready,' she muttered, and ran for the stairs.

Behind her she heard Rob say, 'What's the matter with her?'

'What do you think, Dr Buchanan? She's not made of stone, you know!'

She didn't wait to hear Rob's reply, but went into her bedroom, brushed her hair and retouched her make-up—a defence mechanism, she realised bleakly—and ran back downstairs.

'OK, I'm ready,' she called, and, lifting her coat off the hook in the hall, she struggled to put it on.

'Here, the arm's hooked up,' He was standing right behind her, and as he helped her into her coat she felt the brush of his fingers like hot coals on the nape of her neck.

'All set?' he said gruffly, and she nodded. 'Let's go, then.'

The journey was every bit as nerve-racking as she had imagined. They talked about patients for a while, and she filled him in on the morning's surgery. As she wouldn't be here to answer any questions later, it made sense to pass on all she could. Anyway, it kept them off more personal topics.

When they ran out of shop talk, Rob told her some of the history of the area they were passing through, and then finally they were there and spared the agony of finding idle conversation in the midst of such emotional turmoil.

As he led the way to the ward, Jamie could see the tension building in Rob. She could feel it in herself, too. Would Trudy have started to reject the kidney? It often happened, and, although it could be controlled usually with prednisolone, it was a set-back and a worrying time for the relatives.

However, as they rounded the corner into the ward, their fears were instantly allayed. Trudy was sitting at a table in the middle of the ward with one of the nurses, doing a jigsaw, and as she looked up and saw them her face lit up and she scrambled to her feet.

'Dr Rob! You've come again—and brought Dr Cameron!'

She threw herself enthusiastically into his arms and hugged him, and he gently disentangled her and ruffled her hair.

'Hello, darling,' he said huskily, and gave her a lop-sided grin. 'I can see how you are, anyway. Perky as a parrot. She giving you a hard time?' he asked the nurse.

'Och, no, she's a wee treasure,' the nurse replied with a wide smile. 'Are you her father?'

He shook his head. 'No, I'm her GP, but we see quite a lot of you, don't we, pet?'

She snuggled up to his side and nodded. 'I don't

have a daddy, now, but Dr Rob said if I ever need a home I can go and live with him. Come and help me do the jigsaw,' she said to Rob, and tugged his hand.

He met Jamie's eyes, his own registering the weight of responsibility, hers telling him she was willing to share the burden.

He looked away. 'How's your mum?' he asked the child.

'Oh, she's fine. She's resting today—she knew you were coming and the lady she's staying with didn't mind, so she's spending the day at her house. I don't mind,' she assured them. 'I'm so used to being here it's almost like home now. What's in that bag?' she asked Jamie.

'Oh!' Jamie had forgotten all about the bag. 'It's for you—I hope you like it.'

She handed the bag to Trudy, and watched as she pulled out the contents. It was a jumper, in the same soft heathery blue as her eyes, with little tortoiseshell cats just like Trudy's all over it. She had found it earlier in the week in Fort William, and was so taken with the pictures and the wonderfully soft texture that she couldn't resist it.

'Oh, Dr Cameron, it's lovely! Thank you——'

She flung her arms around Jamie's neck and hugged her hard.

'Steady, you'll split your stitches,' she said unevenly, and, with a gentle squeeze, she released her and turned her attention to the jigsaw. 'Come on, let's see if we can't do some of this sky for you.'

They spent two hours with the little girl, and Jamie had to fight her feelings when the time came to leave.

'Will you come and visit me again?' she asked Jamie eagerly.

'I—I can't, sweetheart. I'm leaving tomorrow.'

Trudy's face collapsed. 'You can't go—how will Dr Rob manage without you?'

Jamie smiled bravely. 'He'll manage, darling. He's getting someone else to help.'

'But he'll miss you!'

'Trudy, it's OK,' Rob said gently. 'I'll cope fine.'

She looked from him to Jamie, and wrapped her arms round Jamie's waist. 'I'll write to you,' she promised, 'and I'll think of you every time I wear my new jumper.'

Jamie hugged her back. Her lip wobbled and she caught it between her teeth, fiercely suppressing the tears that were threatening.

'I'll keep in touch,' she promised, 'and if I'm ever up this way I'll come and visit you. OK?'

Trudy nodded, and Jamie let her go.

'I'll wait for you outside,' she said to Rob, and turned on her heel, walking swiftly along the corridors to the car park.

By the time Rob emerged she had regained control of herself, and managed to give him a weak smile.

'Sorry about that. I hate goodbyes.'

He met her eyes across the car. 'So do I. Come on, let's go.'

They drove back in silence, for which she was profoundly grateful. She couldn't have made small talk to save her life.

When they got back he rang Iain and thanked him, caught up on the current state of affairs, and went out again to see the patient the other doctor had been about to visit.

Jamie picked at a casserole Mrs Harrison had left for them, and decided she might as well go and finish her packing so she was ready to get away early in the morning.

She opened the last drawer and went still. On the top lay Mrs McKay's patchwork quilt, its soft jewel colours blurring with tears.

Picking it up, Jamie cradled it against her cheek and sank on to the bed, flooded with memories. Only seven weeks, and yet there were so many. Mrs McKay, at rest now, whose gentle sweetness would remain with Jamie for ever. Josie and Sandy Reeve and their baby, who so nearly didn't make it because of the storm. She wondered how he would grow and develop over the years. Trudy too, with her transplant and her courage and the tragedy of her mother's failing health—how would she get on? How would her life turn out? Would her mother live? Would she end up with Rob, or would the courts refuse to let her live with him?

Bess too, with her puppy, now a lively and inquisitive five weeks of age and heavily into mischief. She was devoted to Jamie—would she pine without her? If she had had a home to go to, she might have taken Bess, leaving the puppy with Chloe, but she had nowhere, and God knew where she would end up.

And then, of course, there was Rob, her gentle giant, so caring, so tender, capable of such a wealth of emotion but so stubborn and blind where she was concerned. Would he lose Chloe? Dear God, she hoped not. It would destroy him—just as leaving him was destroying her, and it was all so unnecessary. . .!

She turned her face into the patchwork quilt and wept.

Hours later she rose stiffly from the bed and undressed, then crawled miserably under the covers. Time, they said, was a great healer. She wondered how long it would take.

One year? Two? Ten? Or forever. . .

She heard Rob's footsteps on the landing hesitate outside her door, and his voice called her name softly in the darkness. She lay motionless, her heart pounding. It would only take one word and he would be there with her, his body strong and powerful, his clever hands caressing, working their magic, driving her insane with wanting, and then when she was begging, pleading, he would take her, and in that taking give her all she could ever need. . . except his love.

With a muffled sob she turned her face into the pillow and lay silent, waiting for the sound of his receding footsteps. Only then did she dare to breathe again.

Morning found her still awake, her eyes red-rimmed but dry now. She got up and went to the bathroom, showered quickly and dressed in jeans and a sweatshirt and comfy old trainers. She would go to London and cadge a bed from one of her old Westminster colleagues, and then maybe she'd find some locum work with accommodation—preferably working with a woman, to avoid complications, she thought with hollow humour.

She went down to the kitchen and made a cup of tea, drinking it sitting on the floor in front of the stove with Bess leaning on her shoulder and the puppy worrying her shoelaces. She couldn't face food, wanting only to get away. It was not quite seven, and if she made a move soon, she could escape before the house stirred.

And then Rob walked in, dressed in his running shorts, and her heart stopped and then started again with a crash.

'You're up early,' he said conversationally, but she could see the muscle twitching in his jaw and knew he was hating this every bit as much as she was.

'I wanted to get an early start. I have to be in London tonight.'

He nodded briefly. 'I'll go up and sling on some clothes, then I'll give you a hand to load your car.'

She watched him go, then closed her eyes. She really hadn't wanted to see him again. Now she would have to say goodbye. . .

He came down with her case, and put it in the hall. 'Is that it?'

She nodded. 'My medical bag, my coat, my handbag. They're all downstairs.'

Then Mrs Harrison appeared with Chloe.

'All ready?' she said softly.

'As I'll ever be,' Jamie replied, conjuring an unsuccessful smile for Chloe.

'Bye-bye, sweetheart,' she said, crouching down. The little girl, all flushed with sleep, held up her arms to Jamie. Closing her eyes against the tears, she scooped her up and buried her face in the tumbling curls. She smelt of baby powder and warm skin, and her chubby arms tightened around Jamie's neck in a big hug.

'See y'later,' she chirped.

Jamie choked down a sob and hugged her back, then, unwinding the little arms, she handed her to Rob and hugged Mrs Harrison.

'Thanks for everything,' she said unsteadily, and then turned to Rob.

She moved her mouth to speak, but nothing came out. What could she say? He held out his free arm and pulled her hard up against him, lowering, his head and kissing her with all the pent-up passion and emotion of the last two hellish weeks.

And then abruptly he released her, and she picked up her bag and opened it. 'This is for Chloe,' she said, handing him a flat parcel. Then she climbed into the car, reversed jerkily back into the road and drove off, blinking hard to clear the tears. It worked quite well at first, but after about two miles she couldn't seem to blink fast enough any more.

With a ragged sob, she pulled over by the lochside, folded her arms on the steering-wheel, laid down her head and cried.

'What is it?' Chloe asked curiously, tugging at the wrapping paper.

'I don't know, darling. Let's have a look, shall we?' Rob tore open the paper and pulled out a picture frame. Inside there was a photo of Rob, Chloe and Trudy peering into a rock pool. Rob was laughing at something, and Chloe was standing head-down with her bottom in the air, staring intently into the water. Trudy was looking adoringly at Rob.

'She must have taken it the weekend Trudy was here,' Mrs Harrison said.

Rob nodded and closed his eyes. A heavy tear slid down his cheek, and Chloe touched it with her finger.

'Daddy crying?' she said worriedly.

'Why, Rob?' Mrs Harrison asked him gently. 'You allow Trudy to need you, Chloe to need you, Bess and the puppy and the cat, Mrs McKay, me as well—you have love enough for all of us, and yet the one person in the world it seems who can make all your dreams come true you won't allow to need you—or yourself to need her. Because you do need her, you know. Admit it or not, she means the world to you, but you won't let yourself love her, and now she's gone——'

She broke off and bit her lip.

'She was only staying because of Chloe. She didn't really want to marry me.'

'If you believe that then you're a fool, Robert Buchanan—a bigger fool that I took you for. She's been in love with you for weeks, man, and if you weren't so busy hiding from the truth you would have seen it for yourself!'

He stared up the road, as if doing so would bring her back, and then suddenly he shook his head.

'Dear God—Mrs H, will you look after Chloe? If I go now I might catch up with her——'

He handed Chloe over, snatched up the keys of the Land Rover and with a great spurt of gravel he shot off the drive and headed up the road. If he could only catch her before she reached the ferry. . .

* * *

After the first storm of weeping was over, Jamie opened the door and got out. It was still slightly misty, the air cold, and she shivered and turned up her collar, then stumbled down the steep path to the water's edge. There was a little jetty and she walked out to the end of it, oblivious to the broken boards.

Perhaps she should just keep on going, she thought. What was there to stop her? Nobody wanted her, she didn't have anyone who needed her or depended on her—what was the point? She stared into the murky water and shivered. She didn't want to die. Not like that, all alone in the freezing cold water. But living didn't seem like such a bargain either at the moment. Perhaps she would go somewhere like Sudan—somewhere where she would be truly needed. . .

Above her on the road she heard the screech of tyres and then a door slammed, shocking in the stillness.

'Jamie!'

She turned and looked up, just as the sun came over the horizon and cleared the last of the mist.

'Rob?' she whispered.

'Jamie, wait, I need to talk to you!' he called, and he ran down the path, his feet sliding on the loose stones. He skidded to a halt at the edge of the jetty and held out his hand.

'Come here, Jamie,' he said calmly, but his voice was shaking. She wondered why. 'Love, that jetty isn't awful strong—come here, darling. Please?'

Glancing down, she saw the waters of the loch swirling under her feet through the broken boards. Then she looked up at him, and saw the worry and the fear in his eyes, and something else. . .

'Come on, sweetheart. Nice and steady, one step at a time—that's lovely. Keep coming—Jamie!'

The boards crumbled, and she flung her hand out towards him. Then she was in his arms, the jetty matchwood behind her, and he was crushing her to his chest, words tumbling over and over.

'I thought I'd catch you at the ferry, then I saw your car, but you weren't in it. When I saw you standing there on that crumbling jetty, and I thought you were going to kill yourself because of me—dear God, I thought I'd lost you——'

He broke off with a choked sob, and pressed his lips to her hair. His whole body was trembling, his heart pounding under her ear. 'Jamie, I love you. Come home with me, darling. I need you—I can't live without you. I thought I could, but when I saw you drive away. . .'

'Shhh,' she soothed, and tilting back her head, she cupped his wet cheeks in her hands and pulled his face down to hers.

'Kiss me,' she murmured. When he finally lifted his head, she summoned a wobbly smile.

'Was that a marriage proposal, Dr Buchanan?'

His eyes caressed her tenderly. 'If you'll have me,' he said seriously. 'I'm a stubborn, stiff-necked fool, but I love you more than I can say.'

'Keep practising,' she said with a smile. 'You'll get there in the end. And yes, I will marry you. I love you, too, you know.'

'Yes, I know. I'm sorry I didn't believe you.'

'But you do now?'

He nodded. 'You'll have to keep telling me. I have a rotten memory.'

She grinned. 'My pleasure. Shall we go and put Mrs H out of her misery—and then we'd better ring Trudy and ask her to be a bridesmaid.'

He hugged her. 'She'll love that. It's a shame Mrs McKay didn't know.'

"Oh, but she did,' Jamie told him. 'She gave me the patchwork as a wedding present.'

'Wily old bird,' he said fondly. 'She might have told me—it would have saved lot of heartache!'

'You wouldn't have listened.'

He eyed her seriously. 'I'm listening now.'

'I love you.'

He hugged her briefly, and then keeping his arm round her, he led her back up the path to the road.

'Let's go home,' he said gruffly.

It sounded wonderful.

DON'T MISS EUROMANCE

1992 is a special year for European unity, and we have chosen to celebrate this by featuring one Romance a month with a special European flavour.

Every month we'll take you on an exciting journey through the 12 countries of the European Community. In each story the hero will be a native of that country–imagine what it would be like to be kissed by a smouldering Italian, or wined and dined by a passionate Frenchman!

Our first **EUROMANCE**, *'The Alpha Man'* by Kay Thorpe is set in Greece, the land of sunshine and mythology. As a special introductory offer we'll be giving away *'Hungarian Rhapsody'* by another top author, Jessica Steele, absolutely free with every purchase of *'The Alpha Man'*.

And there's more . . .

You can win a trip to Italy simply by entering our competition featured inside all Romances in September and October.

Published: September 1992 Price: £1.70

Available from Boots, Martins, John Menzies, W.H. Smith, most supermarkets and other paperback stockists.
Also available from Mills & Boon Reader Service, PO Box 236, Thornton Road, Croydon, Surrey CR9 3RU.

Mills & Boon